Death Remembers

Wendy Fallon

Death Remembers

Copyright © 2018 by Wendy Fallon

A SHORT ON TIME BOOK:

Fast-paced and fun novels for readers on the go!

For more information, visit the website:

www.shortontimebooks.com

Dedication and Acknowledgments

This book is dedicated to my sister Karen Sharpe who encourages me in everything I do, and who has forgiven me for all the unforgivable things big sisters do to little sisters when we were children.

I thank my cheering squad: Karen Randau, Laurie Fagen, Margaret Morse, Sande Roberts, Katrina Shawver, and Becky Owens from my critique groups; my editor Debbie Kyle, and Head Cheer Leader, Karen Mueller Bryson of Short on Time Books. Thank you also to my husband, Tim, who cheerfully washes laundry and cooks meals while I write. I love you all.

Prologue

Five Years Previous

Two men stared down at the brittle bones littering the bottom of the trench. A yellowish skull with a haunting gap-tooth smile, several long bones, and remnants of cloth and hair lay scattered by the excavating bucket. Splintered pieces of what remained of the back of the head protruded through the exposed eye sockets. The skull grinned with frozen maniacal glee, as if daring them to ignore it.

They both knew the downside of accidentally uncovering human remains. It would set the project back weeks, if not months, until authorities determined if this qualified as a Native American burial site or the scene of a crime. The boss would be livid. After all, they'd already celebrated breaking ground on the project and photos had been distributed to the media.

After a careful examination of the grave and a torturous cell phone conversation with management, they quickly shoveled the dirt back into the trench. The taller man let out a sigh of relief as the appalling grin disappeared under clods of dirt. As they finished, the shorter of the two men held up a small leather bag on a lanyard.

"What the hell is that? Don't tell me you took it from the grave."

"Don't be such a sissy. Of course I took it, and I'm going to split it with you. The dead guy doesn't need it now, right? At least this way we'll get paid."

His pal shuddered and looked over his shoulder to be sure no one watched from the cover of the desert brush, ocotillos and the few boulders large enough to hide behind.

"Well, OK . . . but this place gives me the creeps."

They spent some time brushing the newly turned earth with dry tumbleweed and scattering dead mesquite leaves generously around the gravesite, then shook hands.

As they drove away, one of them looked in the rearview mirror and noted a black, oddly solid-looking mist rising from the grave.

One

Sunday Evening

Paralyzed with terror, I stood rooted to my kitchen floor staring out into the wild, September Phoenix night. My straining muscles and gasping breath spread panic to the tiny dachshund I clutched in my arms. Merry's smooth red-brown fur rippled in waves of shivers that ran from nose to tail every few seconds. Lightning split the sky and she yelped, startled by a sudden crack of thunder directly overhead. Taking an involuntary step backward I hugged her close and the small dog whined, shoving her long nose into my armpit as the windows rattled.

Between the streaks of lighting and walls of pelting rain, the sullen hulk of Devil's Mountain lurked, barely visible behind my house. Palm fronds ripped sideways like black streamers in the howling wind and I could see the dark shape of my hummingbird feeder dancing wildly like a tiny spacecraft. I'd always enjoyed thunderstorms and scoffed at those who feared violent weather, but not tonight. Tonight's storm brought with it an unexpected and terrifying premonition of disaster.

Standing in the kitchen of my tiny home, I tried to wrap its warmth around me like a cloak. It had always been my haven, my safe place. Although located in Arizona and built in the local style of tan stucco with a red tile roof, the inside looked more like a cozy New England cottage. The home sat on one level around a central great room, where the kitchen, eating area and living room flowed into one large space. At night, one small reading lamp beside my favorite spot on the sofa, cast a warm beacon of light. Its soft illumination reached into the corners, just enough to dispel imaginary monsters.

A handful of antiques inherited over the years from my parents and grandparents, and hundreds of books, inhabited unexpected nooks and crannies like old friends. My home served as my retreat when the misery of the world became overwhelming, and where Merry and I had comforted each other after my husband, Charlie, died from cancer two years ago.

But tonight's storm inspired anxiety and fear. The usually soothing golden light from my dependable reading lamp seemed to barely reach the edges of the side table it sat on. Blinding jabs of lightning broke into the unfamiliar shadows that gathered around the edges of my great room. I thought I knew my home well, but somehow, tonight, unfamiliar terrors lurked just out of sight. Every piece of furniture threw threatening shapes against the walls.

The oppressive humidity and very weight of the air had been building, with the sharp pain behind my eyes, all afternoon. Tendrils of anxiety seeped through the slivers of openings around the outer doorframes like fog, invading my place of safety. Anxious and restless, I'd prowled around the house, alternately scooping up my puppy, and then setting her down. As the storm finally arrived, it broke over the sharp peaks of Devil's Mountain and rolling down into my yard like a freight train.

Running parallel to and between my house and Devil's Mountain, the concrete Saguaro Gulch Canal flowed with debris. The entire mountain drained the monsoon water from its crevices, as dirt, sand, rocks, bits and pieces of trees and plants and small animals, rocketed past my backyard. I stared into the night as lightning forked from sky to earth, splitting a nearby tree, and in that second, I saw it.

A figure stood on the far side of the canal in rivulets of muddy water. In the blurred outlines of long wet strands of gray hair, I glimpsed a creased, weathered face with broad skeletal cheekbones. Gray rags hanging from a proud, defiant frame, struggling to coalesce into the silhouette of someone, or something, I'd seen before. Two bottomless, black eyes locked on mine for a brief, terrifying moment as time slowed to a stop. My breath froze. Finally released, as from a spell, I sucked air into my lungs and felt Merry squirming in my arms. The phantom was gone.

I knew this figure, even though I'd only seen it once before. After my previous experience I'd convinced myself that the apparition appeared only by a trick of the light or some atmospheric phenomenon. The last time I'd seen it I'd been sure it blossomed from an over-active imagination, the result of a fevered dream.

Gently placing the small dog on the floor, I hurried over to the oak table I used as my desk and sorted frantically through a pile of drawing pads. Finding the one I wanted, I flipped through the pages, then stopped and caught my breath. I'd recorded the previous vision in a sketch. The same eyes, endless black pools, stared from the page.

Grabbing my cell phone, I rooted through the basket on the kitchen counter with a shaking hand for a business card. I realized I was holding my breath again, and expelled it in a whoosh. Finally locating the card under forgotten sticky notes, assorted nonworking pens and keys for locks long lost, I pulled it out and punched the phone number into my cell.

I heard the connection, the pick-up, and the voice on the other end as if through a tin can, and whispered, "It's back. The mountain spirit is back."

As I paused for breath, I wondered how to explain to anyone that I, California May, well-respected, award-winning Southwest artist, and recent widow, could now see ghosts.

Two

Monday Morning

The next morning pulsing red lights of emergency vehicles flashed through the cracks of my bedroom blinds. They matched the rhythmic throbbing of pain from my headache, still with me from the night before. Merry burrowed deeper into the bed as I struggled out of my twisted nest of sheets and blankets and peeked through the window slats. Devil's Mountain sat brooding in weak patches of pale sunlight, and the sky hung dark and overcast. Although the canal behind my back fence had calmed from the turbulent swell of last night, the washed-out landscape in the predawn light appeared menacing.

I watched, listening to the beep-beep-beep, as an ambulance backed up along the canal. The blinding red lights reflected off the zippered body bag being loaded into the back.

My stomach rolled as I assumed a body must have washed up onto the concrete shores of Saguaro Gulch Canal directly behind my house. In fact, in the exact spot the apparition had stood the night before. This wasn't my first experience with the apparition. The spirit seemed to reside on or in the mountain, and the only other time I'd seen it had come immediately before finding a corpse. Why was I seeing these things? Was I losing my mind?

Thoughts of crawling back into bed tempted me, but at precisely eight a.m. the doorbell rang, accompanied by the frantic barking of my small watchdog. As I looked through my side window, a uniformed officer lifted his finger to punch the doorbell again. Alphonso Gomez, Charlie's former partner on the Saguaro Gulch Police force stood on my doorstep. I recognized the rotund figure in the tan uniform with unruly salt and pepper curls springing from under his hat. Removing it, I knew, would expose a balding crown.

After Charlie died, Al was an occasional visitor. He brought flowers, brownies and cups of expensive coffee. Embarrassed by his few gifts even before Charlie's death, I naively accepted his attention. Ever respectful while Charlie lived, he astonished me one year after Charlie's death with a declaration of love. He stopped by the house with his hat in his hands, and awkwardly bent down on one knee in my kitchen. It was horrifying to know how much I'd hurt him when I refused. He'd rushed off before I could explain.

I had always been thankful that Charlie could trust him with his life. Mostly a sweet, shy man, Al appeared to be a lovable buffoon, until his quest for respect overcame his good sense. His habit of always seeing the world in black and white, and his need to be right, caused friction. Sometimes, though, he simply drove me crazy with his lack of imagination. I knew he didn't understand my refusal, and every conversation with him since had turned awkward and uncomfortable, filled with long stretches of prickly silence. I opened the door and invited him in, praying he wouldn't, once more, beg me to change my mind.

"Hi Cali." He cleared his throat self-consciously. "I need to ask you one or two questions about what you might have seen last night."

He had no idea. I'd never mentioned my recent paranormal experiences to him. I knew he'd never believe me. On the other hand, maybe he'd think me so crazy he'd stop coming around. For a brief moment I toyed with the idea of telling him, just to see the expression in his green eyes, and then reluctantly decided I couldn't. With my luck, he'd decide that much craziness made me the perfect suspect. Staying silent wasn't really breaking the law, was it?

"Come on in, Al. I'm not sure I have anything to tell you."

Stepping over Merry, he gingerly sat on the edge of the over-stuffed sofa, as if afraid to get too comfortable. He was awkward and shy when he'd shown up at the house after Charlie's death. Maybe because I'd totally redecorated it in my inner artist's favorite wild colors of greens, purples and blues, with peach and orange accents. The wooden kitchen table and matching chairs were stained dark plum. I'd always sensed he was uncomfortable around creative personalities, and he'd never mentioned my artwork. I wondered if I'd been added to the ranks of 'hippy freaks' since rebuffing him.

He glanced around suspiciously as Merry gave his shoes a thorough sniffing. Retiring to her doggy bed, conveniently located where she could keep an eye on everyone, she watched him with unblinking eyes.

"Would you like something to drink? Tea, coffee . . . soda?"

"No. I'd really just like to get down to business. Did you notice anything out of the ordinary last night?" I winced at his police voice, as he officiously pulled out his small notebook and pencil.

"You mean outside of the monsoon of the century? It was pretty dark. I assume you mean in the canal?"

"Anything at all, Cali. You never know if you've seen something that might be important."

I hesitated. I had seen something, but I knew he wouldn't want to hear about it.

"Well, I didn't really see anything but a lot of rain, lightning and mud. As I said, it was so dark out there I couldn't really see anything past my fence."

Al's expression sharpened.

"Let me remind you this is a serious investigation. Are you absolutely sure?"

"You know I'd tell you if I saw anything . . . unusual." Well, the ghost was certainly unusual, but not something I could share with him. I looked back at him with wide eyes and hoped he'd believe me. Al sighed.

"OK. If you remember anything, anything at all, just call me as soon as possible. Charlie had my number, but here's my card anyway."

"Of course." I nodded my head earnestly as he made his way to the door. "Um, have you identified the victim yet? Was it an accident?"

"All information is highly confidential at this point. You know I can't tell you anything, Cali. Look, I know you must be lonely without Charlie around, why don't I pick you up for dinner tonight?"

Darn it. He'd almost made it out the door without bringing it up.

"If I thought we could eat dinner as friends, Al, I would say yes. But you insist on making things so complicated. I really don't think it's a good idea." I sighed, knowing he wouldn't understand.

"Well, let me know if you need anything." Al left, his shoulders slumped.

Monday Afternoon

That afternoon, I opened my front door again to find Daniel Silvertree standing on my doorstep. Members of the local Clanewasa Tribe, Daniel and his grandmother had shed a whole different perspective on my first experience with the mountain spirit. He was the only one I'd ever told about my terrifying talent. As an Arizona State Park Ranger, Daniel had come to my rescue after my first paranormal ordeal, which had taken place in Devil's Mountain State Park last spring. It had been on a deceptively sparkling morning in May.

"I'm so glad you could come. I really don't know what to do." I threw the words over my shoulder as I nervously led him into the great room. Moving aside several pillows, along with Merry whose small black nose and tail quivered with excitement at the sight of another visitor, I invited him to sit.

"I'll just get some ice tea," and I bustled off into the kitchen before he could protest.

Returning with a tray with two glasses of unsweetened tea and a plate of cookies, I tried to smile confidently. The glasses rattled slightly as I tried, unsuccessfully, to hide my anxiety.

In one swift movement Daniel arose, took the tray from me and placed it gently on the coffee table. He sat quietly until I sank slowly into the armchair. Both of us ignored the food.

Finally he spoke. As a peaceful man of few words, he filled entire rooms with his soothing aura. I knew I could spend time with him in complete silence and feel totally relaxed.

"You've seen the spirit again." I found his simple statement of fact comforting. "I've already spoken to the officers on the scene. Even though the canal belongs to the utility company, it flows through Devil's Mountain State Park, so they let me ask some questions. An early morning jogger found the body of a man in the canal behind your house." He paused and smiled gently. "The similarities to your previous experience are startling."

How could he possibly sound so relaxed about it?

"How can you be so . . . so calm about it?" A wave of heat rushed up my neck and face and I quickly reached up to push my hair, curling into tiny ringlets from nervous sweat, out of my eyes.

"I mean, nobody really believes in ghosts, do they? And why me? Why am I the one to see him? What does he want from me?" And what if the ghost was the killer? Can ghosts actually harm people? As a measure of my terror I felt more concerned with my possible loss of sanity than the poor soul who had lost his life.

I immediately flushed and ducked my head as my voice trembled. Since Charlie had died I tried hard to be independent. It had been a mistake to tell my thirty-year-old daughter, Sophie, about my previous paranormal experience. She seemed to believe I'd lost my mind, perhaps as a sign of old age. I'd always been organized when we were a family of three, when she was growing up. During my first year after losing Charlie, I'd hardly left the house. And when I did, disaster followed. I would dissolve into tears at the grocery store in the check-out line because I'd left my wallet at home; go to the post office to mail bills I'd forgotten to bring with me; and missed scheduled meetings with her at the Coffee Shoppe. Just as I began to recover from Charlie's death and enjoy the independence of making my own decisions, she threatened to move in with me. I loved her dearly, but acknowledged her impulsive and opinionated nature. I wanted to believe in her self-confidence as a successful, award-winning photographer, but now I wondered if my own breakdown had somehow convinced her she now had to be the strong one. How could I convince her I wanted, and could handle, my own life?

"You remember what Grandmother said the last time?" Daniel looked at me, smiling gently. "You are receptive to spirit, perhaps because you're still grieving for your husband . . ." his voice trailed away as my chin began to quiver.

"I didn't mean to upset you." He rushed to apologize.

I looked away, pulling a tissue from the sleeve of my sweater and blew my nose with a loud honk.

"It's OK, I've got to get past it. Charlie would want me to move on. Besides, that doesn't explain who the ghost is, or what it wants. Or why there was a body behind my house."

"I talked with Grandmother last night. She told me the story again, the one she remembers from her childhood. She believes the spirit is protecting the mountain. She thinks when the mountain witnesses murder, the only way to cleanse it is to bring the murderer to justice. If this is true, then your dead body might be a murder victim."

A snort escaped me before I could muffle it.

"I don't believe in fairy tales." I looked down and realized I'd twisted the tissue into a lump. "Sorry, I didn't mean to sound disrespectful . . . it's just that you're talking about something that's not supposed to be logical." I no longer believed in fairy tales or magic, and if I was truthful, I was beginning to lose my faith in God. I still didn't understand why God had taken Charlie so soon, or why my prayers had gone unanswered, or even unheard.

Daniel thoughtfully sipped his iced tea.

"I can see what I can find out from the police, and perhaps you can ask a few questions around the neighborhood. Maybe learning more about this latest event will help you."

"I certainly don't have anything else to do." I clasped my hands together tightly, my voice slightly bitter with self-pity as I tried to hold my grief at bay. But sometimes it came that way, unexpectedly washing over my carefully built, but still vulnerable, wall of self-defense.

"I may not feel very useful these days, but I do find it easy to be nosy." I tried to smile, but felt it come out in a crooked grin. Charlie would be relieved I had something to keep me busy, instead of bawling over him all the time. Maybe it was time to stop hiding away in my little cottage with my dog and make friends with my neighbors again. I certainly had enough time on my hands. Charlie had left me a modest but sufficient income and along with my own pension I could afford to retire. Unfortunately it left me without the disciplined schedule of a regular job.

Daniel stood to leave, and side-stepping the dancing Merry, made his way towards the front door.

"By the way, do you still have the drawing you made when the spirit first came to you?"

"Oh, yes. I pulled it out and made a copy of it for you already, here it is." I took a sheet of paper from the kitchen table and handed it to him.

"Grandmother asked to see it. She was curious to see what he looked like." Daniel carefully rolled and tucked the sheet into the breast pocket of his uniform. "I'll call you in a day or so and we can compare notes.

I stared after him as he gently closed the front door.

I did feel a bit better. Daniel and his grandmother took these things seriously. Their culture gave them a completely different point of view. One I didn't really understand. Would asking questions of my neighbors, people I hadn't spoken to in several years except for a few, actually give me any answers? What answers did I hope to find?

I used to be interested in my community, and often discussed Charlie's cases with him. He always said I had a knack for asking the right questions. My best friend and close neighbor, Theresa Thornberg, had invited me to attend a neighborhood women's group at the library in a few nights. As Daniel drove away, I decided to accept. For the first time in a long while, I looked forward to getting out of the house. I had to admit feeling nervous, but what could be the harm in just listening, or even asking questions? Maybe I'd catch some juicy gossip that would lead to a killer.

As I turned towards the kitchen, I thought I heard the click of the coffee maker button being pushed to 'on,' just like Charlie used to do for me when he knew I felt stressed.

Three

Tuesday Morning

I shuffled into the kitchen the next morning and I tripped over Merry as she danced between my feet. With a corpse and a ghost on my mind, who could blame me for not paying attention to my feet? And as on every morning since Charlie's death, I could still imagine him at the stove, making scrambled eggs so he knew I'd have a nutritious start to the day. Blinking rapidly, I wrenched open the fridge and addressed the tiny dog.

"You do know where your food comes from don't you, you little smartie?"

I pulled out the can of dog food with its red plastic snap-on lid. My stomach clenched as I took a quick inventory of likely breakfast candidates. Nothing looked good . . . maybe I'd just have coffee and toast.

Having spooned out several blobs of wet dog food into a bowl for Merry, I settled at the kitchen table with the morning newspaper, a cup of coffee, and two pieces of toast. I read the paper as I nibbled and sipped, skipping from headline to headline. With a night of obsessive thoughts about the events of the previous two days, I found it difficult to concentrate on any one article. On the second page, under the City News section, however, a photo jumped out at me. The headline read:

DEAD MAN IN SAGUARO GULCH CANAL IDENTIFIED

I dropped my toast and grabbed the paper with both hands as I recognized the photograph.

Oh my God, it was a photo of my neighbor, Mike Sands. That poor man! My second thought turned to his family. Mike and Patricia Sands, and their teenage daughter Meghan lived just across the canal and further up the mountain.

Forgetting my half-eaten toast and coffee, I jumped up and rushed to pull on jeans, a tee shirt and running shoes. Dashing back to the kitchen, I rummaged in the kitchen drawer for Merry's leash and harness. The little dog had gobbled her own breakfast in seconds, and squirmed in delight.

"Oh, do sit still, Merry. I can't get your harness on with all this wiggling. No harness, no walk!" I spoke sharply, something I never did, and would come to regret later. Merry immediately sat at attention in surprise.

Grabbing my keys and cell phone, I grasped the end of the leash and rushed out the front door. Hurrying down the sidewalk, I turned into a driveway two doors down, and knocked smartly on the kitchen door just before it flew open.

"Oh, Cali! I just knew you'd come by. Have you seen the paper this morning? Did you see Mike's photo?" A small woman with sharp, bright eyes and short brown hair pulled me inside. Everything, in fact, about my best friend, Theresa Thornberg, appeared sharp and bird-like, reminding me of a nervous sparrow.

"Poor Patricia and Meghan! Who could have done this? It can't be anyone we know, can it?" Theresa led the way to her kitchen, her heals tapping a quick staccato on the floor tiles. Deftly filling two mugs with water and slapping them into the microwave, she pulled out a box of tea bags, creamer and sweetener.

"Well, I hope not . . . but sometimes it's hard to know every-thing...about everybody..." I answered breathlessly.

"What do you mean? Mike and Patricia were good people. Well, I mean, everybody has their problems, but who'd want to kill him?"

"How do we know it was murder? Maybe he just slipped and fell into the canal, in the middle of the monsoon. It could have been an accident." I mulled this over in my mind, even as I spoke.

"I suppose you're right." Theresa paused, tapping the counter impatiently with a vibrant pink finger nail until the microwave beeped. "But I have heard a few things."

I sighed and briefly wished Theresa wouldn't gossip so much, but I couldn't help being curious.

"Like what?" I made myself comfortable at the large refinished farmhouse table and settled Merry under my chair, as Theresa brought over two mugs of steaming water. From the pantry she plucked two tins, pried the lids off, and offered me a homemade chocolate chip cookie and a tea bag, and Merry a dog biscuit. Such a flurry of activity told me she was wound tighter than usual.

She finally sat at the table and dropped her tea bag into her own mug.

"Well, I heard they were having money and other troubles, if you know what I mean." her mouth tightened primly.

I stared at her.

"What do you mean, other troubles? What other troubles?"

"Oh Cali, Honey, you've just been living under a rock since Charlie passed." Theresa suddenly blushed as her hand flew up to cover her mouth. "Oh, I didn't mean to bring Charlie up. I am so sorry!"

I took a deep breath.

"It's OK, Teresa, I'm getting used to it. But tell me what you've heard."

"Well, it's just that I ran into Tiffany Marsh grabbing a latte at The Coffee Shoppe a while back and she said she thought Patricia was having an affair. I asked her if she knew who with, and she said she didn't know." Theresa shrugged, but her eyes were sharp with curiosity.

"But that's just a rumor!"

Theresa continued, as if I hadn't spoken. There was no stopping her flow of words once she got started.

"And you know their daughter, Meghan, still lives at home? Doesn't make more than a few pennies at that waitressing job she's got...and with Mike out of work, and Patricia the only one earning anything decent, maybe he killed himself."

I was about to protest when we were interrupted.

"Well, well, hi there, Cali." Theresa's husband, Jimmy, came unsmiling through the kitchen door, bent down and held out a hand for Merry to sniff. "Haven't seen you 'round in a while. Slumming today, are you?" He didn't meet my eyes.

I smiled at him uncertainly. Jimmy had been one of Charlie's neighborhood friends. They'd both hang out barbecuing and drinking the occasional beer on the weekends. Charlie, I, Theresa and Jimmy had gone out to dinner, and then walked to each other's homes afterwards for drinks. Since Charlie had died, Jimmy had changed. He seemed awkward and unfriendly.

"Oh, you know, we were just talking about the article in the paper this morning about Mike."

"Well I sure hope they catch the bastard that did it." Jimmy spoke in my direction. "See you 'round, Cali."

"I'm going out for a while, Love." He gave Theresa a light kiss on the cheek and stomped out, slamming the back door.

"I just don't know what's got into him, Cali. I really think he misses Charlie, and just doesn't know what to say around you."

"Don't worry about it, Theresa, I'm hoping it'll get easier. I'd like to take you up on your invitation to the women's meeting to-morrow night.

Theresa smiled nervously.

"Jimmy calls them the Devil's Women. He really doesn't like me going, says there's enough groups protecting the wildlife around here and this group is nothing but a pack of gossiping women. But, yes, I'll pick you up at seven. You know how strongly I feel about cleaning up the environment."

Merry and I left Theresa and headed for the canal. I needed some time to think, and walking was my favorite thinking activity.

As Merry first dragged me down the sidewalk, then suddenly stopped to sniff and yank me to a stop, I thought about my visit with Theresa.

I wondered why Jimmy acted so oddly. Maybe it's just like Theresa said and he still missed Charlie.

Well, so do I, I thought angrily.

It would be an interesting women's meeting, though.

The "Women of Devil's Mountain" pledged to serve and pro-tect the wildlife and the mountain communities. What could they possibly accomplish? I'd heard the meetings sometimes dissolved into screaming matches. What could they discuss that would be that controversial? I had never wanted to attend before, but now I was looking forward to it. It might be a great way to see what some of the other Devil's Mountain residents thought about Mike Sands' death.

My thoughts were interrupted by the abrupt buzzing of my phone, and I dug it out of my pocket as I walked. Sophie's name shone from the screen. Drat.

"Mom! What's this I hear about a body in your backyard? Didn't I tell you to move out of there? I didn't worry when Dad was alive, but living along the canal by yourself is dangerous."

"Well, I've spoken to the police and they told me I have nothing to worry about." Well, I intended to, and I didn't feel any threat from a human, so technically, this could be true. "And they discovered the body in the canal, not in my backyard. It could have been an accident."

"See? I told you." Her voice rose into a hysterical wail, completely ignoring my words of reassurance. "I'm coming over as soon as I can after work and we're going to talk about my moving in. You can't live there alone."

This had been an ongoing argument since Charlie had died. I'd thought hard about how I felt. I didn't want Sophie moving in. I finally appreciated having my own space, freedom and choices.

"Mom, are you there? Do I need to come over now?"

"Sophie, I am just fine. I really can take care of myself, and you don't need to come over after work. I'd love to visit with you, of course, but you are not moving in."

"I don't understand, Mom. I thought you loved me. I thought we could move in together, and I could help you with stuff like groceries and the bills. You aren't as young as you once were." Sophie paused. "And you aren't the only one who misses Dad!"

And that, of course, could be the problem. Had I been too selfish in my grief? Had I failed to comfort or understand Sophie's needs after her father's death? She and I had never been close. It was Charlie who spoiled 'his little girl.' He couldn't help it, he spoiled both of us. But where I struggled to find my strength and independence without Charlie, Sophie wanted to come back home.

"I miss Dad, too, and of course I love you, sweetie. You know that. But I need my independence, at least for a while." I tried to make my voice as gentle as possible.

"Well, as long as you're alright. I worry about you, Mom."

"I love you too, Sophie. Why don't you come over for dinner?" I paused to remember which night I wanted to attend the women's meeting. "This weekend?"

She agreed, and I thumbed my phone off as Merry and I continued our walk. Small, fluffy clouds ringed the Valley, floating in a cornflower blue sky. The monsoon humidity still lingered. Although I knew the temperatures wouldn't drop below one hundred degrees Fahrenheit until mid-October, I sniffed the fresh, morning desert air in deep appreciation and thanked God for the coolness in the shadows. With Merry trotting happily beside me, I walked down the sidewalk. On either side of the street well-kept desert landscapes of cacti and mesquite trees thrived on drips from buried water systems, and surrounded by pink or white gravel instead of grass. The single level homes were closely packed but well cared for. Modest. Quiet. Most residents in this neighborhood worked during the day.

The development seemed to exist in a little bubble of peace and complete safety in the middle of the urban wilderness. But I knew safety in the desert could be an illusion.

Turning right onto the main thoroughfare at the end of my road I braced myself for the sudden whoosh of cars on their way up and down the mountain. After several dozen yards, I was relieved to turn right again and step into the no-man's land that ran parallel to my back yard on either side of the canal.

The recent rain had turned the dusty top layer of dirt to mud, which would dry and crack under the sun. Black, rushing water came as close to the top of the concrete lining of the canal as it could without overflowing. The few twisted mesquite trees, with their sweeping tendrils of bright green, sparkled with a clean, washed look, as if someone had carefully bathed each leaf. Tiny tufts of dry grass and weeds burst from an otherwise bare expanse of earth. Bits and pieces of paper and odd discarded food wrappers danced along in the breeze and swept by in the swirling current of water. This corridor off the mountain looked as wild as any African savannah. As benign as it seemed, being encompassed by the city limits, I knew this stretch of dirt and mud witnessed hundreds of small deaths every day.

The trash and garbage left behind by humans, I thought grimly as my gaze travelled down the dirt paths lining both sides of the canal, detracted from its natural beauty. As my eyes swept down the canal, I spotted streamers of bright yellow crime scene tape and a police officer standing guard, just behind my house.

The concrete block and wrought iron fence that ran parallel to the canal on either side provided some privacy. It was also hoped to offer limited protection from the coyotes for the housing developments behind them with their manicured, civilized yards.

I laughed to myself. I'd lived here on the canal for 20 years. It served as a footpath between the urban metro areas around Phoenix and the desert mountain wilderness of Devil's Mountain, not only for humans but for the wild residents as well. I'd seen roadrunners, lizards, rabbits, ground squirrels, quail, rattlesnakes and coyotes. And I'd seen death in this no-man's land, roadrunners with the limp, pale bodies of lizards hanging from their lethal beaks; coyotes hunting baby quail and ground squirrels; ravens and red tail hawks ripping apart desert cottontails and mourning doves. This was a gateway to the wild American Sonoran Southwest; wilderness most urban humans took for granted. The wild desert and urban civilization met briefly along this canal and survived in an unwritten, uneasy truce.

Merry began wiggling all over in excitement as we approached the officer.

"My goodness but you do look warm. Would you like my extra water bottle?" I held out the still-sealed, perspiring plastic container and the officer took it gratefully.

"I live right around here. I don't suppose you can tell me what's going on?" I glanced at his name badge and then into his face.

"Sorry Ma'am, I'm not supposed to talk about it." He shuffled his feet in a patch of dried mud.

"Do I need to check my locks at night? I live alone, you see..." I widened my eyes and tried to look innocent and vulnerable. The officer looked at me and then at Merry, her long hotdog body dancing around in circles at his feet, and smiled reassuringly.

"Oh, I wouldn't worry too much, ma'am, just an accident. Looks like the victim slipped and hit his head in the storm. Probably didn't take the flash flood warnings seriously. Some people still don't, you know." The officer looked at me kindly.

"Well, thank you so much, Officer Bradley, I do appreciate it. I'm so glad the police have everything in hand." I gave him what I hoped was an innocent smile, tugged on the leash and turned to continue our walk.

So, what did I just learn? Anything at all?

My chest tightened painfully. Overcome by doubt, I remembered the apparition had appeared close by. I looked around as a wave of fear washed over me and a shiver went up my spine.

What was I doing? I didn't even know where to start. Why should I care so much about this death? Why couldn't my ghost be Charlie, and friendly looking, instead of something so terrifying?

Merry interrupted my wild imaginings with a violent tug.

"Oh, Merry, what are you doing? You know those might be snake holes!"

The little dachshund, her long, slender tail high in the air whipping rapidly back and forth in a blur, had her butt in the air and nose and face shoved deep into a tiny hole in the ground. I saw with relief that the hole was a bit larger than a snake hole, just the right size for a ground squirrel. Merry loved to chase the little rodents, although they were much too fast for her. Looking around, I noticed we were standing in an entire community of squirrel holes, with dozens of openings in the hard-packed earth to escape into. And when a tiny round head popped up several yards away, I knew the creatures were teasing. Merry didn't seem to mind in the least.

"Merry, you come out of there this instant! Come on, you silly beast...what's that you have?"

Bending down I gently pried open her jaws and Merry reluctantly gave up her treasure. I examined the lump of mud-covered stone in my hand.

Hmmm...some child must have lost a toy. It seemed to be a stone with a pale green surface peeking through the mud in tiny patches.

I pulled some clean tissues from my pocket, gently wrapped the stone and carefully slipped it into the pocket of my jeans.

"Let's go home, Merry, I'm exhausted and hot, and your little face is covered with dirt."

As I trudged home, my thoughts spun around in my head like Merry chasing her tail. My new sleuthing hobby wasn't going to be as easy as I thought. All I had so far included a dead neighbor, a seemingly unrelated ghost, one small green muddy rock, a rumor about Patricia having an affair and their poor family finances. But I knew Charlie would've said it was early days yet.

When we returned home I freed Merry from her harness and leash. After stowing them in the kitchen drawer, I pulled the tissue-wrapped nugget from my jeans. Setting it gently on the kitchen table, I filled a small bowl with tap water, and sat down to see what I could do about cleaning it.

As I unwrapped it, the once-sticky mud flaked off onto the table. The tiny sparkle I saw beneath the mud made me want to scrub the stone clean immediately. I forced myself to slow down and got up to collect a few sheets of old newspaper and a wet paper towel. After cleaning up the dry mud, I quickly laid out the paper and sat down again. The stone, sitting in the bowl of water, had slowly started to shed layers of soggy tissue and mud, and now lay hidden below the surface of brown water. Dipping my fingers into the bowl I fished out the stone and gasped.

As my fingers brought the stone into the sunlight I felt a tiny bolt of electricity shoot up my arm. I yelped, bringing Merry to immediate attention, and I dropped the now translucent green object onto the newspapers. As I sat massaging my fingers and arm my mind blanked.

"What the. . .?!" Merry tilted her head, her ears pulled forward like boat sails as I cursed. What was this thing?

I could see the form of a tiny bear standing on four perfectly shaped paws. In his mouth he held a miniature aqua colored fish, and he carried, tied to his back, a sharply pointed arrowhead and several small pieces of pink stone. Coral? Minuscule bits of what looked like inlaid turquoise served as eyes. It appeared to be an intriguing piece of native American art.

I had seen similar small animal carvings before in the local antique mart, but never one as delicately carved as this one. But it wasn't the shape, color, or even the flush of warmth along my fingers and arm, that caught my attention.

In the sudden burst of energy that had erupted up my finger tips, a cloudy image had shot through my brain. It was that of the horrifying entity I'd seen on the canal the night Mike Sands had died. In the next second it had coalesced into the shape and form of an elderly native American, and then dissolved into a gray mist.

The image had only lasted for the blink of an eye, and once more the practical part of my mind screamed in terror. What's happening to me?

"How. . .why. . ." I sat frozen at the table, the only sound coming from the round kitchen wall clock as it ticked off the seconds.

At the same time I couldn't hold back my curiosity. What was this stone? How was it connected to the mountain spirit? Why me?

Jumping up, I quickly grabbed my sketchbook. Working as fast as I could, I did a sketch of my one-second spirit vision. As I quickly laid out the shape of his body, the only real detail I could recall appeared to be a small bag, hanging from a lanyard around his neck.

"I wonder how many lives I've got left, Merry. I feel like I've just lost at least a few. " Merry woofed and came to stand against my leg.

I left the bear to dry on its own, and hunted for something soft to carry him around in. Finally I settled for one of Charlie's old, but clean, socks. After managing to capture the little bear in the sock without touching him, I tucked him into my purse. I wondered what Daniel would say when I showed him the carved animal and described my shocking experience. We were meeting for coffee Friday morning so I could tell him all about the Women of Devil's Mountain meeting. Could I wait that long?

In the meantime I'd spend the rest of the afternoon searching the Internet for art carvings. Settling on the sofa with my laptop, it took only an hour or so to learn my little green bear, described as a Native American fetish, was an amazing find. It'd been missing since 1952.

Four

Wednesday Evening

The next evening after a light dinner, I poked through my closet for something to wear to the women's meeting. I'd spent the day in my art studio. My old painting clothes were covered in rainbow of paint splotches and I smiled as I thought about wearing them to the meeting.

Taking a long look in the mirror, I frowned. Darn it, more white strands of hair! I paused for a moment, and studied the woman staring back at me. The smudges around my eyes and deep lines in my face that had appeared in the months after Charlie's death had faded. Sure, I'd packed on a few extra pounds . . . several actually, as food and wine had helped my through my grief. But the extra weight padding my body had added soft curves to my shoulders, breasts and hips. It was with surprise that I realized I actually felt happier than I'd felt . . . in years.

Merry lay in the bedroom, her head on her paws, where she could see my every move, and I could hear Charlie's words in my mind.

I love you just the way you are.

Giving myself a shake, I spoke to my dog.

"Really, Merry. Yes, I am going out without you. And yes, you, and I, will be just fine." Merry whined. "What do you suppose these women wear to this meeting?"

Finally I decided on comfort over style, and pulled on a pair of clean jeans and a pale peach, knitted tee and sandals. After carefully applying a bit of blush and lipstick, I combed my short honey-blond curls into smooth waves and popped on my favorite gold hoop earrings

Shoving a small pad and a pen and my cell phone into my purse, I grabbed my keys and headed for the front door. Merry stood in the great room and watched, her tail and ears down.

"Don't worry, Baby, I'll be back soon."

Locking the door behind me, I saw the Thornberg's black Lexus pull up. I hoped Jimmy hadn't given Teresa a hard time about going to the meeting with me.

"Well, are you ready to face the devil's women?" Teresa asked with a grin as I climbed into the passenger seat, so much more comfortable than my old Corolla.

"I'm a little nervous, Teresa. If they start throwing knives, take me right home."

"Why in the world would they do that?"

"Well, they may not be too pleased when I start asking nosy questions, like about Mike's death."

"Don't you worry. There's nothing these women like better than to gossip about their neighbors and each other."

I sincerely hoped so as we pulled into the parking lot of the Devil's Mountain Library. The lot held about a dozen other cars. I wondered how many women attended these meetings. Would I know any of them? Would any of them remember me?

Entering through the wide double doors of steel and glass, I remembered a news article when the construction on the building completed. The author praised the sharp-angled rectangular structure with its floating stairwells as 'progressive architectural design'. After a few summers as the local branch of the city library and community college, the city discovered that steel and glass in the middle of the desert created excessively high electric bills because of the necessary air conditioning. Live and learn. It did look nice with such clean lines, but so impractical. It's too bad they didn't make the architect live in it for a year first. I grinned at the thought.

As Theresa and I made our way up the floating stairs, several women walked briskly ahead of and behind us. Theresa nodded to a few of them and led me to the meeting room. I relaxed a bit as I looked around at the other attendees, relieved to recognize a few friendly faces. I also noticed the variety of informal clothing and realized I fit right in.

Everyone sat in chairs arranged in several rows, some whispering to their neighbors, others sitting quietly, waiting for the meeting to start. I'd seen some of these women out walking or jogging along the canal.

Theresa leaned towards me, whispering.

"That's Marjory Redding. She'll run the meeting, she likes being in charge." Theresa sighed and continued in a sober voice. "She's really a bit of a bully."

I studied the generously proportioned middle-aged woman standing at the front of the room, wearing a bright red tee shirt with matching capris. In contrast to her black hair and dark eyes, the red clothes and cherry lipstick were startling. I didn't remember ever seeing her before.

Reminding me of a red rubber ball, Marjory bounced up and down, and addressed the group in an overly enthusiastic voice.

"Hello, everyone, I'd like to welcome you all to this month's meeting of the Women of Devil's Mountain. WODM to those of us who are members. I see we have a good turnout tonight. My name is Marjory Redding, and I am the president. We will now go around the room, so you may introduce yourselves." She smiled cheerfully and turned aggressively to the woman seated next to her. "We'll start with you, Peggy Jo."

The thin, sandy haired woman next to Marjory cowered, but stood and spoke her name softly.

"Peggy Jo Baker, Treasurer."

I studied each woman as introductions circled towards me, until my turn came to stand. As I spoke my name, one woman yet to be identified stared at me, frowning. Her platinum hair swept into a tight twist at her crown and her short, tight gray skirt, matching jacket, with a silk aqua blouse and black high-heeled sandals seemed to identify her as a corporate power employee. Wow . . . not a hair out of place, not a wrinkle in sight. When her turn came, she spoke in a confident, clipped voice and identified herself as Tiffany Marsh, wife of 'award-winning architect, Brody-Marsh-the-third'. It took me a moment to remember, but realized her husband had built this library, as well as their house up on the mountain that overlooked all the rest of us. Glass, steel, and very, very posh.

I also recognized Emily Brennan and waved across the room. Emily and her husband John lived in the next subdivision up the mountain, but I often met her out walking the canal with their enormous mastiff, Winston.

Marjory's voice cut through the buzz of small talk.

"Ladies, as you know we are here to discuss ideas for using the funds we've raised this year. We are committed to protecting our mountain, its wildlife and ecology, but also sharing it responsibly with the rest of the public. Since most of it is already a state park, the state does what they can to keep the hiking trails, and hikers, safe. But we believe we can help. We will now hear from our treasurer, Peggy Jo Baker."

The nervous, soft-spoken woman blushed painfully and stood once again. As the flush left her face, I could see her skin was milky white and free of makeup, and her blond, shoulder length hair so light it looked white, and lifeless. She wore an A-line powder blue skirt that fell below the knee, a white sweater set, and black flats. Her eyes were pale blue and enormous behind a pair of black-framed glasses.

"Yes, well, we now have a balance of $14,502.39," Peggy Jo spoke and sat back down quickly.

Several hands flew into the air, and Marjory nodded to Tiffany.

"I think we should clean up the canal, pave over the dirt paths, and add some landscaping and benches. I think where it meets the hiking trails we should build some decent rest rooms, where they expanded the parking not too long ago." Tiffany sat down.

A low level of chatter broke out.

"Yes, Cali?" Marjory bellowed above the confusion of noise. I stood and waited for everyone to quiet down.

"I know I'm new here but since you mentioned the canal, I was wondering how you all felt about Mike Sands' death this week. I live on the canal and the body was discovered right behind my house. My husband and I know . . . knew Mike, what I mean is, I know his wife, Patricia. Is she a member? " Everyone stared at me. Even Marjory seemed at a loss for words. I guess I had blind-sided them. Should I have waited?

"Well, I really don't have this on the agenda tonight," Marjory finally sputtered. "I really don't think it's an appropriate discussion for this meeting. I don't encourage gossip, Mrs. May."

I had just gone from 'Cali' to 'Mrs. May.'

A babble of excited voices broke into a confusion of half-baked theories and ridiculous rumor-spawning statements. Everyone, it seemed, had an opinion.

Tiffany jumped up. "I'd like to say something. I think the sooner we get the canal cleaned up the sooner the crime rate will drop. I haven't said this before, but I think we should hire an exterminator to get rid of the coyotes that come down off the mountain. They're filthy and dangerous, and I don't really care what method is used." Tiffany flounced back into her seat.

I frowned.

What the heck did coyotes have to do with the death of one of our neighbors? Arizona already had an open hunting season on coyotes, just not within city limits, and since Devil's Mountain State Park was located within the City of Phoenix, our canal coyotes were pretty safe.

Peggy Jo stood up determinedly, and spoke over the group. Everyone quieted so they could hear her soft but determined voice as she looked directly at Tiffany.

"Is that really what this group is about? The coyotes were here first. We're the intruders. And if our money is going to go for killing off inconvenient wildlife, why not exterminate the ground squirrels that burrow into all our gardens or the rattlesnakes that hikers run into on the paths? The coyotes control those populations, you know. And if any of our money does go for any of these things, then I quit!" Peggy seemed flushed with emotion when she sat back down. Tiffany shifted uncomfortably in her chair. The group seemed momentarily shocked into silence.

Theresa tentatively raised her hand and Marjory nodded to her with obvious relief.

"Maybe we could all email Marjory with our suggestions for the next meeting, and she could appoint a committee to weed out the most popular ones. Even though we don't have enough money for it, I wouldn't mind seeing a visitor's center at the parking area at the state park . . . maybe to educate hikers and visitors and locals about the wildlife. Maybe we could purchase some picnic tables or something."

Theresa sat down. I grinned at her, leaned forward and whispered.

"That was amazing! You are a world-class diplomat!"

Theresa grinned back.

Quickly agreeing to her suggestion, the meeting broke up into small groups of women, all talking at once. Marjory invited everyone for cookies and coffee afterwards, and we all converged on a table set with goodies at the back of the room.

I leaned towards Theresa, so I wouldn't have to yell over the noise of multiple conversations.

"Theresa, I've got to run to the ladies' room, I'll be right back."

"You want me to show you where it is?" She glanced over at Emily, who was headed in our direction, her face sober.

"No, I'll find it. You just talk with Emily, see what she says about Mike."

I slipped through the small clusters of women and realized I'd probably miss the juiciest bits of gossip.

"Did you hear about Suzanne . . . ?"

"Her husband just got laid off . . ."

". . . hit her daughter with a spatula . . ."

I smiled as I thought I would have been tempted to spank a much younger Sophie with a spatula if my husband had just been laid off. I could just imagine Suzanne, whoever she was, snapping under the stress.

"It'd be nice to do something for the Sands family . . ."

Well. At least someone in the crowd was thinking compassionately. I couldn't believe Mike's death had been so easily brushed aside. I was beginning to see that perhaps most of my neighbors preferred to live in their own bubbles of safety, determined to ignore anything unpleasant.

All those thoughts abruptly fell away as I stepped into the cushy silence of the carpeted hallway. A 'Ladies Room' sign pointed the way at the end of the corridor with an arrow to the right. I walked as quickly as I could and shoved the restroom door open with my palm, and froze.

Two voices lashed out at each other. Luckily the restroom had an entryway, and the speakers couldn't see me. From their conversation I doubted they even knew I was there.

"What do you mean, you have it with you? In your purse?" Marjory's voice rose into an escalating shriek. "You stupid, stupid girl!"

"Well, yes. It's perfectly safe. I'll be going by the bank immediately after the meeting. Why should I have to make all those trips out of my way to get to the bank? It's right next to the library, which might be convenient for you, but since I've got this new job you know I live further up the mountain."

"But, Peggy Jo, it'll be dark, you'll be using the night deposit. What if you get robbed, or attacked or worse? I'm telling you right now, if that doesn't get into the bank immediately I'm going to fire you and appoint someone more responsible!"

"You wouldn't! You can't fire me, I'm a volunteer. Nothing will happen to the money, or me. Besides, I always carry my little helper with me." I could hear the sneer in her voice. It seemed underneath all that shyness was an inner core of steel.

Marjory squeaked. Whatever Peggy Jo's little helper was, Marjory hadn't expected it.

"You carry a gun?!" Marjory spoke in a loud whisper. Obviously they weren't afraid of being overheard. I wondered what Peggy Jo might do with her little helper if she found me eavesdropping. Very slowly and quietly I backed out, my need to use the facilities completely forgotten. By the time I'd found Theresa again, everyone was leaving.

Twenty minutes later, Theresa dropped me off in my driveway. Despite the rush of adrenaline and wanting desperately to talk over the events of the evening immediately, we decided to get together the next day. Theresa didn't want to cause any ripples at home by returning late. A rejoicing bundle of smooth fur and flying paws met me as I unlocked the front door. I made a beeline straight to the bathroom to take care of business. After that, I settled myself on the sofa with a pad of paper and a pen, a cup of tea, and a biscuit for Merry. Snuggling down next to me, she burrowed under a pillow and pulled the biscuit after her.

I wrote down all the names I could remember. I hadn't found out if Patricia was a member of WODM. I wondered if she was friends with any of these women or if Mike was?

Marjory Redding, President of WODM, blustery, bully.

Peggy Jo Baker, Treasurer of WODM, passive aggressive, carries a gun, irresponsible.

Tiffany (husband Brody, 'award-winning' architect) Marsh; wants to 'kill off' all the coyotes, and have rest rooms built by the state park parking area.

Emily (husband John) Brennan, John an archeologist with ASU

After a moment, I added:

Theresa (husband Jim) Thornberg, friends of Mike and Patricia's

I wondered if any of these people had anything to do with Mike, Patricia or Megan Sands? Was this a list of the Sands' friends and neighbors...or suspects? Should I add Charlie and me? That was ridiculous. Charlie was dead, and I knew I didn't kill Mike.

I reminded myself sternly that the police hadn't yet determined if Mike's death was murder, or an accident.

I recalled what Theresa had said about what Tiffany had said and added a line.

Patricia, Mike and Meghan Sands: Mike dead, Patricia possible affair, family strapped for money. Meghan a waitress.

I wondered for a second if my daughter Sophie knew her, or had gone to school with her and scribbled.

Megan and Sophie?

Then I erased it. I would have known if Sophie had ever been friends with Megan, and talking to my daughter about her would mean I'd have to explain why I was asking. I didn't want to go down that road unless I absolutely had to. If Sophie found out I was investigating a neighborhood murder, she'd panic. My independence would disappear like a puddle of water in the desert.

Suddenly too tired to read through it again, I yawned widely. Setting aside my notebook, I put my empty mug in the sink and got ready for bed. As Merry and I snuggled under the bedding, my mind churned and wandered. I wondered if Brody Marsh would want a rest room project. Why would an 'award-winning' architect want such an insignificant contract . . . although a visitor's center might be right up his alley. I also wondered why Tiffany thought Patricia was having an affair. I'd see what Theresa thought tomorrow. Had it been an accident, or could Mike have really been murdered by someone we knew?

"Good night, Charlie." I whispered, and felt his soft kiss on the top of my head.

Gasping like a fish out of water, I sucked air into my lungs, gripping the damp bed sheets with both hands. The nightmare had followed me out of sleep and into my bedroom. I lay there, petrified and sweating, listening to the blood pounding in my ears. I awoke, but the terror of the dream, which had seemed so real, still lingered. I couldn't remember it.

Glancing at the clock beside my bed, I couldn't read the time. My vision blurred, and the room swam with moving shadows. The dark shapes in one corner seemed solid, not the wispy, colorless forms of a night without moonlight. As I stared, Charlie stepped out of the darkness. I knew I was still dreaming. Behind him stood a second shadow. The mountain spirit.

Choking in an effort to force out the words, I tried to warn him.

"Don't be afraid, Cali, he is a friend." Charlie's words did little to diminish my terror. "This is the only way he can show himself to you. You must listen to him."

What seemed to be a shapeless, black mist, slowly became the outline of an elderly man. His face was broad across the high cheekbones, and he held himself stiffly, head high. I could see through him, so I assumed he'd been dead much longer than Charlie. Did ghosts fade with time? Holding out his hand, I could see two tiny animal carvings in his palm. He opened his mouth to speak, a sad, beseeching expression on his face. I couldn't understand any of the words he spoke.

"Charlie," I whispered. "Charlie, why visit me now, after all this time? Why have you waited so long?"

"You didn't need me until now. I love you . . ." His words faded into silence, and both shapes grew more and more insubstantial, until they disappeared altogether.

"CHARLIE! Come back . . ."

I must have fallen into a deep sleep, because I opened my eyes to sunlight peeking around the edges of my blinds. Thinking over what I could remember of my nightmare, I realized with a start that the tiny carved animals the spirit held in his hand were identical to the green bear Merry had found on the canal. And the mountain spirit was the elderly Native American I'd seen when cleaning it.

Five

Thursday Morning

On Thursday, after rushing through my morning routine, I picked up my phone.

"Hi Theresa, come on over. I'm ready."

Exhausted and on-edge, I then buzzed around the kitchen staying as busy as possible to avoid thinking about my sleepless night.

Filling the kettle with water, I set it on the stove to heat, and pulled out two mugs along with tea bags, milk and sweetener. Setting the mugs on the counter, I arranged the other items on my purple kitchen table and added my notebook and a sharpened pencil. I threw a dog biscuit into Merry's bed, hoping the she would stay quiet and out of the way. Even though this morning's sunrise had brought with it a return to normality, I was feeling nervous, cranky; like my brain might explode at the smallest hint of a cross word.

As expected, however, Merry started barking frantically as my neighbor approached the front door. I ran to answer it, only to find Al Gomez on my doorstep. Theresa arrived just behind him.

"I've got questions for both of you ladies. We've had an event." He walked into the house and headed for the kitchen before I could invite him in. I shrugged my shoulders as Theresa looked at me in surprise. Al made himself at home at the head of the kitchen table, removed his hat and invited us to join him. His swaggering confidence ticked me off, and with my nerves still raw I felt an angry retort begin to build in my brain. Clamping it down, I struggled to be patient.

"Peggy Jo Baker was mugged last night at the Saguaro Gulch Bank night deposit. She says," he paused and looked at each of us, "$14,500 was taken. She's got a pretty big bump on the head."

Theresa and I stared at him, my anger momentarily defused as I quickly reviewed the previous evening in my head.

"What I want to know is how many people knew she planned to make that deposit? Peggy Jo says she saw you, Cali, walking down the corridor from the Ladies Room to the meeting room, after she and Marjory had a discussion about it."

"Well, yes. I did overhear them arguing. But that doesn't mean I hit her over the head and stole the money, Alphonso Gomez!" I snapped in reply, my spine stiffening.

He'd professed his love once, and now he accused me of assault and theft?

"If neither Marjory or I did it, maybe Peggy Jo did it herself and stole the money."

"That's ridiculous. She's got a bruise and a lump the size of an apple. How could anyone do that to themselves?" Was that a smirk I saw? I couldn't believe what I was hearing. He was taking Peggy Jo's side over mine. I had to admit it would have been a pretty nervy thing for Peggy Jo to pull off and I had no idea why she'd want to. But I was past making sense and so angry I sputtered.

"You'll just have to take our word for it, won't you? Have you got any evidence we were anywhere near her?"

"Well, no. I just wanted to know if you had heard anything." He looked sheepishly at the mugs and the plate of cookies. I gripped my pencil so hard it snapped in half, sounding like a gunshot in the middle of the momentary silence.

"You have a funny way of showing your concern, Al. And don't think I'm offering you any refreshment. You can just close the door gently on your way out." I stood and pointed to the front door. He rose slowly and jammed his hat on his head. Theresa and I stared at each other and cringed as the front door slammed after him.

"Whew! What was that all about?" Theresa looked at me expectantly.

"I forgot to tell you last night on the way home what I'd overheard in the Ladies Room. For whatever reason, Peggy Jo didn't feel it was necessary to deposit a years-worth of WODM money until last night."

"Al's right in one respect," Theresa pointed out. "Someone knew about it, and knew when she would be making that deposit."

As Theresa settled at the kitchen table, I ground my teeth and consciously relaxed my shoulders. Pushing my notebook towards her, I went to pour hot water into the mugs. What could I do about Al? We bickered like an old married couple. Until he'd proposed, I hadn't any idea he had feelings for me. I doubted he'd proposed just because Charlie had asked him to keep me out of trouble. He brought me flowers on occasion since Charlie's death. The memory of my visitors the night before, however, banished all thoughts of dealing with Al.

"Hey, what's this?" Theresa jabbed her finger at the page.

"What?" I set the two mugs on the table and leaned forward.

Theresa pointed to my list of names, specifically her own and Jimmy's.

"I can't believe you'd even think for a second that Jimmy and I had anything to do . . . "

"No, of course not!" I interrupted. Having forgotten I'd added their names, I shook my head vigorously. "This is just a list of everyone I know that knew Mike Sands."

"Still, it's a bit of a shock . . . I don't know if I should be offended . . . I mean we've known you and Charlie for what . . . 20 years?"

"I know you had nothing to do with it."

I didn't know about Jimmy, of course, but I could confidently say that Theresa had nothing to do with Mike's death. I figured I knew her well enough to know that she couldn't have.

"Look," I pointed to the remaining names. "We know these people, we can talk to them, and they won't mind us being nosey. If we put together a flyer about the vote on spending the WODM funds, assuming they're recovered. . . and go knock on doors and ask for opinions, it'll give us the perfect opportunity to find out what they know about the Sands family."

I took a breath and hesitated.

"You could at least talk to Jimmy, and maybe ask if he's ever worked with Mike . . . "

Theresa raised her eyebrows as I continued.

"I mean they've both worked locally in construction, right? Maybe he could tell us if he's seen Mike lately. It's not that we think he did anything . . . "

I closed my mouth abruptly as Theresa bounced up from the table.

"Look, Theresa, for all we know, there are several people with a motive to kill Mike. That doesn't mean Jimmy was one of them.

But we've got to start somewhere, and Jimmy was in the same industry."

Teresa clutched her mug with both hands, and I could see her knuckles turning white. Finally she loosened her grip, set the mug down gently and sank back into her chair.

"Why are you so crazy to find out how, or why, Mike died? It's not like you, or even Charlie, were close friends with him."

I'd been wondering about this myself. She was right. I hadn't been close to the Sands family. I didn't know anything about them. As Merry and I had walked by Mike's last spot on Earth on the canal yesterday, I'd been shocked at how normal everything looked.

"When I looked at that spot on the canal, I didn't see anything. No blood, broken branches, marks on the concrete. There's nothing there to show he was alive one minute and dead the next. I just felt I should be able to see or feel the violence of whatever happened. It's almost like he never existed. No one deserves to die just because he pissed someone off, and right behind my house!"

Not to mention the creepy warning the night before his body turned up. I didn't think Mike was in the canal when the monsoon blew through with its terrifying ghost. The nightmare I'd had last night hadn't reassured me in the least. But I couldn't tell my friend about any of that. Not yet.

Theresa looked at me thoughtfully.

"OK, I guess I see your point. I'll talk to Jimmy about Mike. I'm not happy about it though."

I hurried to reassure her.

"Really, it shouldn't be too hard and it's not because we suspect any of these people of anything."

"I guess that depends on what they say, doesn't it?"

I sighed. What a horrible thought, to suddenly think that one of our neighbors could be a murderer. If it was murder.

Thursday Afternoon

After Theresa left, I ate a quick peanut butter sandwich and hunted up a clipboard. I typed up a few questions on my laptop about the proposed cleanup of the canal and how the Women's group funds could be used. Reluctant to admit they might not be recovered, I determined to move ahead with my own investigation. Convincing the women that I confidently believed the police would find the money wouldn't be hard. They'd want to believe the money could be recovered. Although, judging from the way Al's investigation seemed to be progressing, that wasn't going to happen any time soon.

Looking through my clip-art, I chose an image that looked mildly official for a logo and placed it at the top of the page. A black shield, centered over the forest green outline of a mountain, looked quite impressive when I added 'W. O. D. M.' below it. Adding three choices with checkboxes below the logo about how to spend the WODM money, I felt pleased with my efforts as several copies flew out of the printer.

I'd just say I volunteered to take an opinion poll.

Locking Merry inside the house, I climbed into my aging Corolla and drove off. As I turned into Emily Brennan's sub-division further up the mountain, I wondered about Theresa's reaction to asking Jimmy questions. What did I know about Jimmy Thorn-berg?

On the surface, Jimmy treated his wife like a queen. I'd never seen them argue. He often gave her gifts, took her on trips, and kissed her every single time I'd seen him leave their kitchen. They lived in a small, but beautifully decorated home and drove a new, expensive car. Theresa's clothes and hair were always elegant. In the last couple of years, however, I'd noticed they didn't actually look each other in the eye. And Theresa never contradicted her husband. Ever.

Emily answered my knock. Emily and John Brennan lived in a small development similar to my own. These houses were two stories rather than my single floor, but the desert landscaping in the front yard boasted the same broken pink gravel and heat-resistant plants. Their very large dog, Winston, and a small white cat sniffed my pant legs and shoes in the foyer. Emily banished them to another room as she invited me in.

"This is a nice surprise, Cali. It's wonderful to see you."

Emily was in her mid-thirties, tall and slender, with a ready smile.

Whenever I'd seen her, Emily always seemed to be happy with her life.

"Come on through to the kitchen. Can I get you a cold soda, or ice water?"

"A soda would be nice."

Emily placed two glasses with ice on her kitchen island and pulled two cans of root beer from a gigantic fridge.

"Let's take them into the den, it's much more comfortable."

In reality, the den and the kitchen combined to make one large room divided by the kitchen island. Up-to-date stainless-steel appliances and black marble countertops shone spotless at one end, and a flat screen TV was mounted on the opposite wall. Floral, overstuffed armchairs and a sofa arranged on a red area rug facing the TV made an inviting space. The tiled floor and painted walls of pale gray made a soothing backdrop, cool colors for the Phoenix summer heat. On the outside wall French doors opened onto a patio and I saw a brilliant patch of green lawn surrounding a sparkling clear swimming pool.

As I sank into an armchair, Emily settled onto the sofa and pulled her legs up under her. We both popped open a can, poured the refreshment over ice, and savored a first sip.

"So, how are you, Emily?"

"Oh, you know, with John working long hours at the University I've had a lot of time to get projects done around the house." We briefly discussed wall finishes and paint colors before I finally got around to the reason for my visit.

"Emily, do you or John know the Sands family?" Impatient to get down to business, I'd completely forgotten the clipboard tucked away in my purse.

"Well, I know Pat certainly. She's a member of the Women of Devil's Mountain group. I saw you there last night. Your first visit?"

"Yes, Theresa invited me." I hoped Emily wouldn't ask about my sudden interest in the group. "I guess I'm just trying to get out of the house more since . . . since Charlie died."

Shocked, I realized I'd said this out loud for the first time.

Emily nodded her head, and looked sad.

"Well, that's the only time I ever see Pat, but of course I see Meghan at the Coffee Shoppe all the time." She paused. "What happened to Mike is so awful! They kept to themselves, though. I don't think they were close to anyone."

I liked Emily. Her compassion for a family she hardly even knew was obvious.

"Why are you asking?"

Ready for this question, I felt I could trust her.

"I'm investigating Mike's death. I don't think it was an accident."

Emily set her glass on a side table, un-tucked her legs and leaned forward.

"But I thought the police had already decided it was an accident."

"I know, but . . . someone else," or something else, "believes it was murder, and . . . asked . . . me to look into it." I shivered as I thought of the mountain spirit.

"Why you?"

Good question. If I knew what this spirit wanted, and why it chose me, I'd feel a whole lot better about grilling my neighbors.

"Well, I'm not sure. Maybe it has something to do with Charlie being a police detective."

I wondered where that brilliant piece of reasoning came from. Although, now that I thought about it, Charlie had discussed his cases with me. Had I actually helped him?

"I suppose that makes sense." Emily looked at me. "You know, I always wondered why Mike left the construction business. He and Pat always seemed to be short of money."

"He left construction? When?" I wondered if a better question might be why.

"Well, you know that John is working at the University in the Archeology department." No, I didn't know that, I thought to myself, wondering at the relevance. "He had a dig planned for Devil's Mountain about five years ago, but the University pulled the funding at the last minute. I seem to remember John saying not long after that he ran into Mike. Seems Mike had been fired from a contract job with that big construction company, Timmons Development. Meghan told me her dad worked at the Lumber Yard in town now."

Emily turned and called up the stairs that led off the den.

"John? Cali's here . . . come on down and say hello."

I listened as John thumped his way down the stairs and poked his head around the corner of the stairwell.

"Well, hi there, Cali! What brings you up the mountain?" With 15 years between them, they always surprised me with their strong relationship. Their love for each other shone clearly through every expression, conversation, and body movement. They leaned into each other. I wondered what had brought these two people together.

"Cali was asking if we knew Mike Sands." Emily looked at her rumpled husband fondly. John matched her in height and slenderness, with a thick, wild thatch of brown hair. The skin around his eyes crinkled attractively when he smiled. I'd always thought of him as ruggedly handsome.

John sat next to his wife on the sofa and draped his arm around her shoulders. They were obviously very much at ease with each other.

"Let me think." John frowned for a moment. "He did some work for George Timmons. 'Bout five years ago Timmons proposed a Visitor Center for Devil's Mountain State Park, and I think Mike was part of the crew hired to expand the parking lot. He might have even started trenching for the utilities. For some reason Timmons cancelled the contract, and the whole project fell through. Something ridiculous about expansive soil."

John reached across his wife, grabbed her glass and took a swallow before continuing.

"I ran into Mike in the parking lot of the Lumber Yard soon after and he told me he'd left construction." John frowned.

"I did years of research into the Native American tribes of the Southwest and I am absolutely positive an ancient community exists on Devil's Mountain." He shook his head in frustration. "But they pulled my funding right around the same time, and they still won't tell me why."

Leaving Emily and John I climbed back into the baking interior of my car. Sitting with the engine running and the air conditioning on full blast, I quickly wrote down everything I could remember of our conversation.

Looking at my mobile phone I realized it was almost five in the afternoon, but I thought I could make it to Tiffany's and back before dark.

Tiffany and 'Brody-Marsh-the-third', the 'award-winning' architect, lived at the highest elevation homes were allowed on Devil's Mountain. It was no secret that Brody had designed their home, as well as the Devil's Mountain library. Both had been the subject of numerous magazine photos and articles. Although I knew his buildings were hailed as the cutting edge of architectural design, I just couldn't like either structure. Glass and metal are so impractical in the desert.

I finally reached the turn to the Marsh home, marked by concrete and glass pillars on either side of the drive. A decorative concrete wall disappeared into the mountain crevices to either side of the entrance, and I assumed it encircled the entire property.

As I came around a curve, the house thrust itself from the mountain and over a deep ravine. The steel and glass construction had been cantilevered out into seemingly thin air, making the building look as though it was floating. The mountain reared up behind it, blocking the low sun. Brilliant rays of sunset shot through the rugged crevices from behind the house, tipping the ocotillo and saguaros with gold. With its back to the mountain in the day's ebbing light, the front of the house sat in dark shadow. This explained the blaze of light pouring out of every window. No curtains blocked the view, into or out of the home.

I hadn't called ahead. I wondered if they'd see me, or if they were even home. The place appeared to be lit up like a Christmas tree, so I decided someone must be there to answer the door.

I parked in the wide driveway, and approached the impressively large entrance. Knocking sharply at the double entry, I turned to admire the view. To my right the city of Phoenix lay spread across the valley floor in streaks of orange sunset and black shadow.

"May I help you?" A cool, disapproving voice asked as I turned back.

Before me stood Tiffany Marsh, platinum blond hair perfectly coiffed and wearing a dark plum silk sheath with black heels. I was immediately painfully aware of my own jeans, tee shirt and sneakers.

Tiffany showed no signs of recognizing me, nor did she look like she'd be inviting me in. Whipping out my clipboard, I plunged into my presentation.

"Hi Tiffany! I'm Cali May, from the Women of Devil's Mountain meeting last night and I volunteered to poll all the members about how our funds should be spent. I'm especially interested in your opinion about cleaning up the canal. May I come in?"

"I—I'm terribly busy at the moment. Why don't you call and make an appointment when I'm better able to give you my full attention?"

"Well, I'd love to, but Marjory—you know Marjory Redding, our president—wants your feedback as soon as possible, and you were so eloquent last night that I put your name at the top of my list." I gave her a wide, toothy smile with what I hoped was an expectant look.

"Oh, I guess I was, wasn't I? Why don't you come in and I'll fix us both a little drink." Tiffany beamed at my shameless flattery and patted her impeccable hair. "Come right this way."

This was beginning to be fun. For the briefest moment I allowed myself to believe I might have a flair for detecting after all.

As I followed my hostess down a marble-floored corridor and into what looked like a huge snow globe, I realized the snow was wall-to-wall white shag carpet. The room had three walls of glass overlooking the city. The fourth wall had been covered in a gigantic photomural of a forest of beech trees under a full moon. Modern furniture of steel and white leather sat scattered around the over-large space like marbles, thrown down by a bad-tempered pre-schooler. As Tiffany settled onto one of the sculptured chairs, she created the unlikely image of a peacock gently coming to rest in a snow bank.

Clapping her hands, she demanded two chocolate martinis from the gray-uniformed woman who appeared. I shouldn't have been surprised that Tiffany employed help, but I wondered why her maid hadn't answered the front door.

I watched as the dark-haired, petit woman returned with our drinks, placed them on the glass table between the chairs and quickly disappeared back down the hallway without a word. Tiffany tucked a wayward platinum hair behind her ear and answered my unasked question.

"That's just Rosa, my sometimes maid." I raised my eyebrows.

"Sometimes she listens, sometimes she doesn't. Now, what would you like to know?"

This time I played my part and sat up straight on the cold, uncomfortable seating, clipboard in one hand and my pen in the other.

"You may not know this, but I live right on the canal. We've been having so much trouble with the coyotes coming off the mountain, and then a dead body turned up." I silently apologized to my wildlife friends.

"Oh, yes. I am so in favor of cleaning up the canal. Those nasty wild dogs are so vicious and dirty, I'll bet they mauled that poor man." Tiffany gushed with enthusiasm at the thought of destroying the troublesome beasts, but I quickly jumped in.

"Oh no, we don't . . . I mean I've heard the police don't have any reason to believe the man was killed by a wild animal . . . but maybe if we built a visitor's center, to educate the residents about the mountain and the canal . . . "

"Well, yes, I suppose that might help, but I really think they have to lift the hunting ban within city limits and that would get rid of those filthy animals . . . and of course Brody would design the visitor's center. Brody's forever bringing home books about the wildlife around here, though. Ugh. You're welcome to borrow a few if you like." Tiffany pointed to a stack of artfully arranged books on the glass table that held our drinks.

"Um, OK . . ." I leaned over and took the top two books without reading the titles. Returning them might be a good excuse to come back if I needed to.

Even as I shuddered in horror at what the woman was saying, I began to realize that Tiffany had already had more than enough alcohol. I'd better get my questions in before she became completely knackered.

"Tiffany, did you know the police have identified the victim as Mike Sands? Did you or your husband know him?"

Tiffany choked as she swallowed a sip of her drink, then grabbed a napkin to cover her mouth.

"No, I hadn't heard that! I, of course, only knew him by sight."

I hadn't expected her to know him. He'd have been a working peon in her bling and alcohol fueled world.

"But I think he might have worked with . . . I mean, for, my husband. I seem to remember he worked in construction . . . and Brody's an award-winning architect, you know.

I smothered a sigh.

Tiffany smiled blearily in my direction.

"I do feel like a little nap. So sorry, can you show yourself out?"

As I watched, Tiffany closed her eyes and curled up on her chilly sculpted chair. I wondered if alcohol was her only vice. Had I seen the glitter of an additional indulgence in her eyes?

No one came to show me out, but as I looked down the hallway I saw the flash of a white skirt. The maid had worn a gray uniform. Had someone else been listening to our conversation?

Setting my drink, of which I'd only had one sip, down on a side table, I quickly collected my clipboard, purse and the borrowed books and stood up to leave. As I looked around the room I saw a standing glass display case I hadn't noticed when I arrived. Arranged in neat rows, on several glass shelves, and lighted from above, a small army of Zuni fetishes caught my attention.

Six

Thursday Night

Arriving home after my visit to the Marshes' I decided on an early bedtime. But climbing into bed and settling in with Merry wasn't as reassuring or restful as I had hoped. All I could think about was the previous evening. Looking into the corner, I could picture both Charlie and the spirit. What was I thinking? They were both spirits! I finally fell into an uneasy sleep, hoping Charlie would come again, but leave his friend behind . . .wherever that was.

Friday Morning

On Friday morning I jumped out of bed feeling rested and optimistic. Surprisingly, I had slept the entire night without interruption or dreams. Daniel had asked me to meet him at the Coffee Shoppe for breakfast. Clearly he wasn't the reason for my change in mood, but as I selected my clothing for the day, I carefully avoided my usual worn-out but comfortable jeans and shapeless tee shirts. Pale green cotton slacks and a matching blouse would do nicely.

Why did I suddenly care about what I wore? This must be a sign of something positive, right? I had to admit I looked forward to getting out of the house.

My mind lingered for a moment on Daniel before I firmly shoved him to the back of my mind. As attractive as he was, I'd never admit he could be the cause for my early morning enthusiasm. Charlie's sharp eyes floated through my mind. I still thought of my husband every day, and probably would for the rest of my life. Why did I feel guilty?

When I arrived at the Coffee Shoppe fifteen minutes early, I tucked myself into a corner with a large coffee and a cinnamon scone. As I waited for Daniel I watched Meghan Sands wipe down tables. Why did I care so much about the death of her father? Was it simply because no one deserved to be obliterated from the world before their time, or was the mountain spirit egging me on? What exactly did the ghost have to do with Mike's murder? I realized that I had decided it must indeed be murder, and not an accident. I still hadn't decided if the spirit represented good or evil, or anything at all, but at least thinking about it no longer gave me the shivers.

I mentally reviewed everything I had discovered, including the tiny green bear I could feel through the sock in my purse. If I believed in my own night terrors, and the green bear was indeed related to the carved animals I had seen in my dream, it would be totally unbelievable. The nightmare could easily be a creation of my own overactive imagination, perhaps caused by the very discovery of the animal carving along the canal. Daniel slipped quietly into the empty chair next to me. Distracted with my own thoughts, I hadn't even seen him arrive.

###

We both stared at the small green bear sitting in the center of the cafe table between us. It had tumbled gently from the sock as I explained where and when I'd found it, and what had happened when I'd cleaned it. As I pulled my sketch book out and turned to the drawing of the elderly Native American surrounded by a dark mist, I described the shock of energy I'd experienced. My fingers tingled at the memory.

"I know it looks like a Zuni fetish. What I don't understand is how it got into a ground squirrel hole beside the canal, directly behind my house . . . ten feet from a dead body."

Daniel finally reached out and gently lifted the tiny stone animal between his thumb and forefinger. Still he was silent. His gaze sharpened as he examined the animal's belly.

"There are initials carved into it, most likely those of the artist." He glanced up. "I can do some research and find out more. But in the meantime this little guy needs to be turned over to the police. They won't be happy you held on to it, you know."

"How can it possibly be related?" I watched as Daniel set the bear down, pulled out his phone, and began photographing the fetish from every angle. He didn't answer right away.

"I did find out a few things . . . " He left the sentence hanging as he tucked the bear back into the sock and then into his shirt pocket. I watched it disappear and wondered if I would ever see it again.

"The police have confirmed it wasn't an accident. Michael Sands was hit on the back of the head with something heavy or hard enough to crush his skull. They also found a leather lanyard nearby. You know, traditionally these fetishes were carried in a small leather pouch worn around the neck. It may be that he or his murderer wore something like that when he was killed."

I felt the blood drain from my face, and closed my eyes. This detecting business no longer felt like a game; this was real and I felt my stomach twist. We sat quietly for a moment while I pulled my mind back from the awful scene of what must have been Mike Sands' last moments of life. I silently pointed to the small leather bag and lanyard in my drawing, but neither of us could think of anything to say.

"Well," my voice wobbled, "talking about fetishes, I saw an entire collection of them at Tiffany and Brody Marsh's home." I quickly explained how I had attended the women's meeting, and visited a few of the attendees. I ended in a whisper as Meghan Sands cleared the table next us.

Amazed at how soon she'd come into work after her father's death, I guessed she and her mother needed the money. Poor kid. I thought about calling the girl over, treating her to a beverage and asking how she and her mom were doing, but Meghan turned away with a haunted, glazed look.

I leaned forward.

"I spoke with Tiffany Marsh and Emily and John Brennan. John's an archeologist and Brody Marsh is an architect, and they've both worked with, or knew of, Mike Sands when he was in construction. He did excavation or something. Then about five years ago he got himself fired and ended up working at the Lumber Yard in town."

Daniel sat quietly for a moment, taking in the information, then spoke.

"I wonder what happened five years ago? Did Charlie keep any records of the cases he was working on when he left the force? He retired just about the same time, didn't he?"

"Yes . . . but he didn't keep anything that I know of. I'll look around though."

It wasn't until I finished off my coffee and we were walking out into the parking lot that I realized he hadn't commented on my most recent experiences, or my sketch.

As soon as I arrived home from the Coffee Shoppe, I began to search. Had Charlie left anything behind? How could he have possibly known I'd need it now, this long after he'd left me? So often since his death, I'd felt him in the house. Just out of view, in the next room, or hidden in the shadows at night. I wished he'd give me some direction, anything that would help me understand what was going on. The nightmare didn't count, because it simply didn't make sense.

Pulling everything out of one closet, then another, I slowly but systematically tore my house apart. It was a long shot, but if something illegal had been going on locally five years ago, Charlie would have known about it.

Two cheese sandwiches, three cups of coffee, and six hours later, I found it. I had searched every closet, every room, all the cabinets and drawers, and the garage. And found nothing remotely related to the Sands family. I didn't even know what I was looking for. It took hours to shove everything back into place. After the first hour of frustration, I simply threw whatever I couldn't deal with into the trash.

As I sat on the sofa to drink the last of my third cup of coffee, I tried to relax my aching neck and shoulders. Merry inched her way up beside me and laid her head in my lap. As I stroked her soft fur I slowly looked around.

Whew! My house was cleaner than it had ever been, but I hadn't found a thing. My efforts left only one more place that I could think of. The attic.

An unfinished crawl space, the attic was reached through a tiny square opening in the ceiling of my walk-in closet.

We had never put anything up there because of the deadly heat in the summer, and the pigeons that always found a way in. Too exhausted to wonder why Charlie would've hidden anything in such a hole, I decided I'd better look anyway.

With the last of my caffeine-fueled energy, I dragged the ladder from the garage, through the kitchen, living room, bedroom and the bathroom, and into my closet. Grumbling out loud the entire way from the garage, I yelped when I banged my thumb between the ladder and the doorframe to my closet. I thought of a few choice words for the architect of my own house.

At least I now knew where to find the flashlight, which I took with me.

With the flashlight in one hand, I climbed the ladder and pushed up the square of plywood that covered the hole in the ceiling. After a small avalanche of dust and cobwebs and a flurry of sneezes, I poked my head into the intense heat of the attic. Tiny slices of sunlight filtered through the vents from the outside creating a play of shadow and light in which spirals of dust motes danced. I immediately saw the shoebox. It stood out as the only thing up there, except for the air conditioning unit, and had been pushed just out of reach along one of the rafters.

I had to pull myself onto the highest step, lean out, and grab the box. With a sigh of relief I quickly retreated down the ladder.

Merry gently poked her nose into the back of my legs.

"OK, OK, Merry, I know it's time for you to eat." I set the shoebox, dust and all, on the kitchen table and threw some kibble into her bowl. The dog sat in the middle of the kitchen and stared at me.

"Oh, for God's sake. You are a silly beast." I added a bowl of clean water, and a few spoons of wet dog food on top of the kibble. "You are so spoiled. Do you know that?"

Merry woofed and happily settled down to her dinner, tail wagging, as I returned to the box.

Taking it, I settled onto the sofa and slowly lifted the lid. For one insane moment I thought Charlie might pop out of it . . . and I wasn't far wrong.

Sitting in an unorganized pile inside the box were photographs and news clippings. Right on top sat a note written in Charlie's scratchy handwriting, and folded into quarters. Seeing his penmanship couldn't have hit me in the heart any harder than if it had been Charlie himself.

The tears began before I could even reach in and pull the note out with a shaking hand.

###

Dearest Cali,

I knew you were the one the first time you opened your mouth and asked who I was. A very deep and fascinating question it turns out. Only you would know I'd been struggling with it all my life. I will always love you, even after the end. If you are reading this, you now know the diagnosis is fatal. I will be leaving you soon, but there are so many lose ends. You've got such an amazing way of asking the right questions, I'd never have solved half the cases I did without your quirky mind!

The bits and pieces in this shoebox are clues I've found along the way, answers maybe to questions not yet asked. Or perhaps they pose their own questions to mysteries not yet uncovered. Each item snagged my attention in some way that I can't explain. They are pieces of puzzles surrounding the Mountain. They don't call it Devil's Mountain for nothing.

I've hidden this box in case whatever it holds is dangerous. After knowing and loving you and sharing 30 years of life with you, I know you are the only one who understands my passion for solving crimes, especially murder. . .

And I believe each piece in this box points to someone who died before their time, at the hand of another human. Each hides the unforgivable act of taking a life.

Only the murderers will know if these bits are the keys to unexplained death, and if they know you have them, you will become their next target. If you decide you've had enough of solving my puzzles, I completely understand. If so, please give this box to my old partner, Al Gomez. He'll know what to do with it.

You will always be my dearest, and I would never willingly place you in danger,

Your loving Charlie

I sat crying on my overstuffed sofa for some time, one arm around Merry and one cradling the shoebox. The letter lay open on my knees. Finally digging into my jeans pocket, I pulled out a wadded tissue, blew my nose and dabbed my eyes. I could taste salt at the corners of my mouth.

After several deep breaths I resettled myself and began to explore Charlie's mysterious artifacts. Most of them were newspaper clippings, mixed with a few photos. Nothing caught my attention until I lifted out a news photo, and recognized Mike Sands. He stood dwarfed in the shadow of the backhoe parked behind him, and next to him stood someone whose face I couldn't make out. The newspaper reproduction of the photo looked smudged and worn, and the names were cut off the bottom. Turning it over, I found the words "Devil's Mt., Sands +?" in Charlie's handwriting. Flipping it back over, I looked closely at the unidentified figure. Something about the height, shape or maybe the pose seemed familiar.

Replacing the news photo and closing the lid, I gently pushed Merry to one side and got up to find my pad and pen. I then sat at the kitchen table over a ham, cheese and mustard sandwich contemplating my notes.

It was time to visit Pat and Meghan Sands, pay my respects, and take them some food. I knew there wouldn't be anything I could say to them that would truly make a difference or alleviate the pain of their loss. But maybe they could answer a few my questions.

###

Saturday Morning

Saturday morning dawned muggy and hot—a typical Southwest September day. Hopefully it would take another couple of days before the humidity and moisture from Mexico burst into billowing monsoon clouds. The sun was still low over the peaks in the East, sending streaks of sunlight down the length of the canal and striping my shadowed backyard. The low angle of the sun made this the best time of day for a walk.

Merry and I set out, keeping to the shade as much as possible to take advantage of the cooler shadows.

The police tape had disappeared and there were no signs of the violent event from the week before.

Jimmy gave a curt nod from his backyard as we walked briskly by along the canal.

The neighborhood seemed back to normal. You wouldn't even know someone had died here. I shivered as I came even with the crime scene, and Merry whined and pulled on the leash to avoid stopping. As I slowed and stared at the concrete shores of the canal, I couldn't see anything out of the ordinary. Bothered by the thought that Mike's last moments had been so quickly cleaned up and swept away, I couldn't believe there weren't any signs of his death. I felt sad that the violence of ripping his life from him didn't leave some kind of mark on the universe. Maybe the ghost, or mountain spirit or apparition, or whatever I'd seen, had been not only a premonition, but an acknowledgement by the universe of Mike's lost life.

As I walked, I remembered the words of Charlie's letter.

He'd written "especially murder. . ." Murder. Well, yes, we'd solved a few murders together, but I never thought I'd been that much help. The image of a stabbing victim flashed across my mind, and the body of a poor man, shot in defense of his home. I'd helped Charlie solve both those cases. Of course, taking note of details with an artist's eye, like the evidence I'd uncovered in Charlie's most famous murder case ten years ago had given me immense satisfaction.

Did I have a fascination for murder, or could it just be a morbid obsession with death? I'd always believed in something after death, but where had Charlie gone? And did it matter if death came naturally and peacefully, or violently and not according to God's plan? Why did the God I'd been raised to trust allow murder victims to die before their time? I had to solve Mike's murder. I had to find out why someone had taken his life prematurely. What could possibly justify it?

Of course, now I couldn't think about Mike's death without seeing the horrifying apparition that had preceded it. Had it been a warning of violent, unnatural death, or an expression of outrage?

I decided to stop by on my way home and ask Theresa if she'd come to Pat's with me. There had to be something we could learn, that perhaps Pat would tell us and not the police. We were neighbors, after all.

As I glanced up, I found Jimmy watching me from his backyard with a frown. I waved and smiled at him. This time he didn't acknowledge me, but turned abruptly and disappeared into the house.

On my return, Merry and I walked up the driveway of my best friend and knocked on her kitchen door. After several minutes Theresa answered it, but stood in the doorway, not inviting us in.

"So I wondered if you'd come with me to Pat's. We could take some food and pay our respects."

Theresa fidgeted in the doorway, blocking my view into the house.

"I just don't know, Cali. I don't think I'm cut out for all this detective stuff. Jimmy's home today and I thought I'd spend time with him."

"Ah, OK." I was baffled. "What's gotten into you, Theresa? You're usually up for anything."

She shrugged and looked away.

"Jimmy says he doesn't want me sticking my nose in. He says it's dangerous and I should just mind my own business and let the police handle it."

"For Goodness' sake, we're just paying a neighborly visit."

"Well, I'll talk to him and give you a call after lunch." Theresa lowered her eyes and quietly closed the door. Merry and I slowly walked down the sidewalk toward home.

What would bother Jimmy so much that he wouldn't allow Theresa to visit her neighbors? Maybe he just felt concerned. I had to admit Mike's death would be the first murder our neighborhood had ever experienced. How would Charlie react if he were here? He'd practically given me permission from beyond the grave to investigate. I knew Jimmy worshipped his wife, so maybe he just wanted to protect her.

As I reached my own front door, I heard my cell phone ringing inside. I rushed to unlock and open the door, and realized with a jolt that I'd forgotten to take it with me. I never went anywhere without my phone. Did my forgetfulness signal a slow descent into old age? Theresa responded at the other end to my breathless greeting.

"Listen, Cali, Jimmy's gone out for the rest of the day, so I think I'll come with you to Pat's. I managed to convince him we were just going to take food and hold her hand. There's one thing you've got to promise me, though. You can't ask me any questions about what's going on with Jimmy and me. I don't want to talk about it...at least not yet."

"Um, OK . . . I promise not to ask. But you'll let me know sometime, won't you? You know I'd help you in any way I can."

"I don't think there's anything anyone can do."

Hearing a slight tremor in my friend's voice, I felt a vague flutter of unease. Bound by my promise, I reluctantly dismissed my fears.

"I'll let you know what time I'll be by to pick you up. I'm going to call Pat to ask if she'll see us, and put together a meal to take over.

At four in the afternoon I parked at the end of my neighbor's driveway and Theresa hurried to join me. Settled into the backseat sat a covered dish of baked spaghetti and meatballs, a plastic food container of mixed green salad, and a loaf of garlic bread wrapped in foil. Comfort food, with lots of carbohydrates and calories. Theresa carried an unopened bottle of red wine to go with it.

I thought back to my own first days after Charlie died. Nothing had made me feel better. But drowning the pain in carbs and wine had been mindless, and certainly better than doing nothing. I sincerely hoped the meal would provide Pat and Meghan a small amount of comfort.

Returning my thoughts to the friend sitting in my passenger seat, I felt tense and awkward, and apart from a brief comment on the building humidity neither of us spoke.

Seven

Friday Evening

"Hi Pat, we just wanted to come by to see how you and Meghan are doing, and offer our help, if you need it . . ." I stood awkwardly at the Sands' front door. Theresa stood behind me, her arms full of dishes. "We brought you food." I gestured with the garlic bread loaf in Theresa's direction.

I knew in my heart my words sounded totally inadequate. Why did I think mere food would make a difference? Because the only alternative would be to say or do nothing at all, and I, better than most, knew how painful it could be when friends stayed away.

Pat smiled weakly and opened her front door wider.

"Oh, thank you, Cali, Theresa. I haven't felt like cooking or eating much." Her smile faltered. "But I appreciate the thought."

Leading us past the small living room on one side, and the dining room on the other, we found ourselves in a cozy kitchen. Meghan rose from the tiny round kitchen table and flashed a faint grin.

"Meg, this is Cali and Theresa. They've brought dinner for tonight. You can eat before you go into the Coffee Shoppe." Pat looked at her daughter hopefully.

Meghan wrinkled her nose.

"We'll see, Mom."

"She hasn't eaten a proper meal since . . . since Mike . . ." Pat swallowed.

Theresa and I quickly busied ourselves tucking the dishes into the fridge.

Pat wiped her eyes with a dishtowel and offered ice water and tea. Soon all four of us were seated around the tiny kitchen table sipping iced tea.

"Have the police been by?" I asked casually.

"Ha! Several times. I don't think there's a question they haven't asked." Pat sighed.

"I saw you at the Coffee Shoppe with the park ranger the other day." Meghan glanced at me shyly.

"It surprised me to see you were back to work so soon."

"Yeah, well, it keeps me busy, and we need the money. I saw the little green bear you gave him."

I blinked.

Meghan continued, her voice dropping to a whisper.

"Dad had one just like it."

I sat stunned for a brief moment before finding my voice.

"Oh dear, I'm sure it can't be the same one, Meghan. They're pretty easy to find all over the Southwest." I hoped Meghan would believe me. "Where did your Dad find his?"

"I don't know. He used to pull it out every once in a while and tell me it was his good luck charm. Only I guess he wasn't so lucky, was he?"

Her voice cracked as she stood abruptly and rushed from the kitchen. I looked at Pat, stricken.

"Pat, I'm so sorry! I didn't mean to upset her."

"Oh, it's OK, Cali." Pat waved her hand in Meghan's direction. "Everything reminds her of Mike. It's going to take a lot of time for both of us I'm afraid."

"I know this might be hard to talk about, but it might be important to know if Mike's green bear is still here in the house."

"Well, I'll look for it and let you know. Oh dear. What am I going to do? I just feel so guilty!" Pat grabbed the dishtowel as tears began to slide down her face.

Theresa jumped up from the table and began rummaging around in cabinets and drawers, while I patted Pat ineffectually on the arm.

"It will get better, I promise." I couldn't think of anything better to say. "I know it hurts now, and you have to cry about it. That's part of the healing."

Even as I said the words I knew they were hogwash. They had said the same thing to me, but the pain didn't ever go away. In the next moment I wondered why she felt guilty.

Theresa appeared again with three glasses of red wine and a plate of warm garlic bread.

As we sat quietly munching on crisp, savory bread and sipping wine, Pat slowly calmed down, her tears easing to a stop.

"Here's my cell number, you can call me any time." I scribbled my phone number on a scrap of paper out of my purse. "Let me know if you find the bear, or if you need anything at all. I had a really hard time when Charlie died."

Pat accompanied us to the front door.

"Thanks again, for thinking of us."

As we stood awkwardly silent for a moment, I impulsively reached out and enveloped Pat in a brief hug, my heart breaking for this family. It was hard indeed to lose a loved one.

###

"Wow, how sad." Theresa whispered and crushed a tissue in her fist as we drove home.

"You must remember what a basket case I was over losing Charlie."

"But with Charlie so sick for a such a long time, we all knew he wouldn't make it. Doesn't that prepare you even a little?"

I glanced at my friend in astonishment. Was there a pre-defined, acceptable period for grieving after the death of a loved one? Is this what people thought of me—that I'd wallowed in my loss long enough? That after two years everything was OK again? I shrugged and answered her question.

"I thought it would, but it didn't. It was the worst experience of my life."

Theresa crossed her arms and hugged herself, abruptly changing the subject.

"So what's this about a green bear?"

I sighed.

"I found a small carved stone bear, or rather Merry found it, out along the canal."

"And you didn't tell me?"

"I honestly didn't think it was important. And besides, with everything else happening, it slipped my mind."

Theresa stared at me.

"Cali, don't you trust me?"

I couldn't believe it.

"Well, Jimmy certainly doesn't trust me. When have we been able to get together and talk lately? You told me this morning you weren't even sure you were 'cut out' for detective work." I pressed my lips together angrily and then continued.

"You can't have it both ways. You want me to tell you everything, but you don't want to help, and your husband doesn't even want us to see each other."

I made an effort to relax my shoulders, and glanced over at Theresa again. My friend sat in the passenger seat, staring at her hands clutched tightly in her lap.

"Sorry, Cali."

"No, it's my fault. I'm sorry for snapping. This murder has just got us all on edge. The sooner we find out what happened to Mike, the better. The last thing I want is to force you, my best friend, to choose between your husband and me. Give me a call when you can, Theresa, or come on over for tea anytime."

I watched as she climbed out of the car and walked up the drive, her head down.

I felt the strangeness the minute I pulled into my driveway. Turning the car off, I sat for a moment staring at my front door, the neighborhood frozen in absolute silence.

And I suddenly knew, as my heart constricted, that it shouldn't have been this quiet. Why wasn't Merry barking?

"No, no, no...!" I whispered to myself as I approached my front door. It stood slightly ajar. My little dachshund should be barking her head off, her little furry body wiggling in joyful welcome. I had always suspected Merry could hear and recognize the sound of the Corolla from at least a block away.

Pushing the door open, I began to panic and rushed into the living room. Running from room to room, calling Merry's name as

I went, I finally came to a halt in front of the back door. It, too, stood ajar.

The hand printed note in block letters, and taped to the inside of the glass, confirmed the fear building in the pit of my stomach.

KEEP YOUR NOSE OUT

OR YOU'LL END UP LIKE

YOUR DOG AND YOUR HUSBAND,

DEAD!

"No...!" I tore the note from the window, stuffed it into my jeans pocket and sprinted into the backyard. I heard a faint, small sound.

After a frantic search of the gathering shadows around my yard I stood at the back fence and listened. A high-pitched yowling cry came from the canal. Even worse, a dark, swirling mist arose from the black water. Water that seemed unusually high.

I knew the water shouldn't be this high and tried to remember what I knew about the canals, even as I placed my foot on the top of the two-foot concrete block base of the fence. I had no choice but to climb over the additional four feet of wrought iron railing. I'd never done it before, but didn't hesitate.

I just knew it was Merry crying in the distance. Hoisting myself up with my arms, I swung a leg over the top of the fence and tumbled, limbs flailing, into the purple sage bushes on the other side. After struggling a moment to get myself disentangled, I rolled awkwardly into the dirt and stood up.

By now the sun had set and the canal had become an inky black writhing ribbon of water. The mist still swirled and hovered and I knew if I allowed myself any time to think about it I'd become paralyzed with fear. I recognized the mountain spirit, and its warning of impending death. I didn't even contemplate the fact that my reaction to this unexplained phenomenon had changed from debilitating terror to anger and a blind determination to change the outcome. I plunged into the darkness towards the thin frantic cry. The spirit egged me on, racing me, and just out of my peripheral vision, to reach my dog first.

"Merry, I can hear you. Where are you, sweetie? The water is rising...you can't be in the canal, can you? Oh, please God, please, let her be OK!"

Stumbling along in the dark, I felt my foot drop into a ground squirrel hole and fell to my knees. Scrambling to stand, I continued to hobble down the side of the canal, ignoring the pain. My subconscience made a list of details.

"Theresa and Jimmy's place on the left. A firefly? No, it's a lit cigarette. Is Jimmy watching me? Main road up the mountain straight ahead. Water in the canal backing up. Merry's still crying."

Still the spirit raced beside me, pushing me forward faster than I thought possible on a twisted ankle. I felt it's overwhelming presence pushing me forward. On some level I was aware of the smell of age like that of an old musty library, with waves of rage and frustration radiating from its core. It rose from the canal in a blackness that blotted out the night sky. I ran faster.

Just beyond Theresa's house, I found her. Merry fought against the rushing water, caught up against one of the metal grates that spanned the canal periodically to control the water flow. The animal seemed unable to climb or rise above the unusually strong current, and struggled, pinned against the grate.

I didn't hesitate. Clambering down the sloping concrete sides of the canal and into the rushing water, I immediately lost my footing. Managing a gulp of air before going under, I came up seconds later against the grate and right beside my terrified dog. As I reached out to grab Merry I realized two things. The first was I could touch the bottom of the canal with my feet and only the strength of the rushing water pushed me off balance.

The second discovery froze my heart. As I grabbed Merry to pull her up, the dog wouldn't, or couldn't move.

"Oh, my God, your leash is tied to the grate. It's below the water. I'll never get you loose in time."

Even as I began to panic, my fingers felt frantically around the dog's collar until I found the clip for the leash. It slipped out of my hand twice as the rushing water forced its way into my mouth. I struggled to keep Merry's nose above the water with my other hand.

Just as my feet were once more swept from under me and the animal's nose disappeared below the black turbulence Merry came free and landed in my arms. We tumbled together like clothes in a washing machine, before I felt strong hands grab and lift me to safety. I still grasped Merry tightly to my chest, my eyes and mouth clamped shut. Fingers gently pried the animal from my grip as I began to cry.

"You're OK, Cali, everything is OK." Theresa's soothing voice whispered in my ear. Blankets were wrapped around my shoulders as I began to shiver.

"Merry. Where is she? Is she hurt?" I just couldn't imagine what would have happened if I hadn't arrived home when I did. I couldn't stop shaking or crying.

"Cali, open your eyes. Merry's fine, but it was a close thing." Jimmy's voice broke in.

As I opened my eyes I saw paramedics, Theresa and Jimmy, and a small gathering of neighbors. Lights from an ambulance flashed red and several concerned faces peered into mine. A strong paramedic stepped into sight carrying a bundle of blankets. He grinned at me and carefully set the bundle in my arms and pulled back a fold. Two bright eyes stared back at me and the bundle wriggled weakly as I leaned in for a doggy kiss.

As everyone began to leave, I looked down the canal. Even in my gulping, terrified state I noticed the black mist had receded from the canal and the desert night sky twinkled with a million points of starlight.

Friday Midnight

"What the hell have you gotten yourself into, Cali?" Al roared as he stared distractedly at the crumpled wet noted I'd carefully pulled from my jeans pocket.

After refusing to go to the hospital, I sat at my kitchen table at midnight. The paramedics had finally wrapped my sprained ankle, swaddled Merry and me in blankets, and taken us home. After rushing to the scene and then to my house, Al joined me in the kitchen. I had showered, changed and called Daniel. He also sat in the kitchen. Theresa and Jimmy had been persuaded to leave my side and return to their own home.

With Merry in my arms, I sat with Daniel and Al around my kitchen table with mugs of hot coffee. Merry was munching happily on a piece of toast she'd stolen from a plate sitting between us. No one even noticed.

Now that I could think, I found I couldn't stop shaking. Several items littered the table between us. The news clipping from the shoebox and the tiny bear fetish had joined the threatening note.

Daniel picked up the news clipping and examined the accompanying photo closely. I had not revealed the shoebox. It still held the letter and the last items Charlie had thought important and I wasn't ready to share them yet. Al continued to study the note I'd ripped off my back door. I sat lost in thought as wave after wave of shivers ran through my body.

"Why would anyone want to hurt Merry?" I still couldn't believe it. Daniel shifted uncomfortably.

"As a warning, I think. It looks like you've spooked someone." He pointed to the note. "Definitely someone wants you to stop asking questions." His eyes were dark with concern.

"You have to stop whatever it is you're doing, Cali." Al's fist hit the table, making us all jump, but I saw the concern in his face.

"But how do I know which of my neighbors did this?" I realized my shivers were disappearing, replaced by anger. "I haven't uncovered anything but more questions. None of it makes sense."

Daniel looked thoughtful.

"Well, what do we know?"

I began to tick off facts on my fingers.

"We know that Mike Sands worked in construction as an excavator five years ago, with Timmons Development on a site on Devil's Mountain. He was fired right about then. Both Brodie Marsh, architect, and John Brennan, archeologist, worked with him at various times. All three of them got shut down on Devil's Mountain projects. Brennan was planning to excavate an archeological site for Arizona State University. Marsh was designing a visitors' center, which was funded by Timmons Development. Sands was contracted to enlarge the parking lot and trench for the utilities for the visitors' center. What does that news clipping tell us?"

Daniel looked at it.

"Nothing we didn't already know. And the photo is so badly reproduced we can't identify anyone but Mike. The names have been cut off."

Al sat looking at the note.

"I hate to say this, but this note makes me think something else happened as well. He read it out loud.

KEEP YOUR NOSE OUT
OR YOU'LL END UP LIKE
YOUR DOG AND YOUR HUSBAND,
DEAD

"Why would the writer refer to Charlie?" I frowned.

"It almost sounds as though this person had something to do with . . . No. It couldn't possibly be . . . Charlie died of natural causes...didn't he?"

I looked from Al to Daniel in horror. Both men looked grim.

Eight

Saturday Morning

After a sleepless night, I climbed out of bed once again with a blinding headache. Every muscle hurt. It was Saturday, and it seemed like I had a million things to do, but really didn't feel like doing anything. I gasped as I put weight on my ankle and the pain brought tears to my eyes.

This was ridiculous. I couldn't hobble all over with this ankle. Al was right, my wings had been clipped. I wouldn't be barging into anyone's kitchen asking questions, at least not today.

"Maybe it's time to relax, knock around the house, and get a load of laundry done, maybe do some drawing, right Merry?"

The dog opened her eyes at the sound of her name and peeked at me from under a mound of bed covers, but didn't move.

I crawled back into bed and gathered Merry into my arms.

"You poor thing! I'm so sorry you got caught up in this, it's all my fault! I'll call the vet today and see if he can make a house call and check you over. I will never complain about your barking, or picky eating...or begging...or anything, ever again!"

As I hugged Merry tightly to my chest, I felt a few tears meander down my face and fall from the tip of my nose.

"Oh, Merry. I'm so selfish sometimes. It never occurred to me you'd be in danger. But some monster knows you're my dearest and closest friend. How am I going to keep you safe?"

I lay back and relived the events of the past week. At what point had I lost control of my life? Had all of this started only a few days ago, or had I slowly lost my mind over the two years since Charlie's death?

Now, of course, I knew why Merry hadn't been barking. The past week had culminated last night in the horror of rescuing my tiny four-legged child from the sucking waters of the canal.

I thought back to the conversation with Al and Daniel the night before.

"Are you absolutely positive it was intentional? Could Merry have gotten loose and got her leash caught . . . ?" Al asked.

I shook my head vehemently.

"No. Someone had to get into the house, put the leash on her and tie it in a double knot to the underside of the grate." I shut my eyes and shivered as I remembered following the leash with my fingers from Merry's collar to the heart-stopping discovery of the knot.

"Hm . . . we'll need to go back and retrieve that leash. I'll see if one of my guys found it, and where." Al blushed. He'd been so concerned about me that he didn't know if the leash had been recovered or not.

"That makes it malicious intent to harm . . . which along with the note makes you a target." Al's voice was grim.

"I think we'd better review everything you've done since the murder, any notes you've made, who you've spoken to . . . "

"Maybe we should come back tomorrow." Daniel suggested.

I sighed and nodded. *Oh Charlie. How I miss you.*

Now, in the bright light of morning, I felt barely able to get out of bed. Snuggling up with Merry, I closed my eyes and immediately fell asleep again, aching, sore and exhausted.

The thudding and ringing came from a distance as I slowly struggled awake a couple of hours later. Groaning, I rolled over, got slowly to my feet, and hopped to the front door. My ankle still hurt like blazes.

Peeking through the side window, I saw Al, fidgeting impatiently on the other side of the door.

"I was beginning to think I'd have to break in . . . " Al started as I let him in. Right behind him stood Daniel.

As they walked through the living room, I waved vaguely in the direction of the kitchen.

"Help yourselves, make tea or coffee, toast, there may even be some eggs." I hadn't been to the grocery store in over a week, and frankly hurt too much to care.

"I'm going to take a hot shower and a few painkillers. Be with you in a bit." I grimaced and hobbled toward my bedroom.

As I struggled to get dressed after a nice long shower, I could smell bacon, eggs, and fresh coffee. I felt much better as I sat down to a table piled high with plates of breakfast, steaming mugs, and notebooks.

Wow. Maybe we were a real team. Could I be 'one of the guys?' My aches began to fade.

After a silent few minutes of devoted attention to our food, the two men cleared and stacked the dishes in the dishwasher as I sipped the last of my coffee.

I glanced sideways at my companions and smothered a grin.

Charlie in the kitchen, cooking, making breakfast for Sophie and I on a weekend morning, flashed across my mind. I could get used to this. Again.

Finally all three of us sat at the table, notebooks open. Merry lolled in her doggy bed, where she could keep an eye on everyone.

Al spoke, at once stiff and awkward.

"As the investigating officer into the death of Mike Sands, I can't share what we've uncovered, but you two are obligated by law to tell me everything you know. I'm sure I don't need to remind you we could be doing this downtown at the station."

I looked at him in disbelief.

What a pain! You'd think by now he'd know neither Daniel nor I could be suspects. But I supposed he had to do his job.

I spoke up.

"Can you at least confirm some of our assumptions?"

"Look, Cali, you know I can't guarantee anything. If there are facts that have already been made public, I don't see any harm in passing it along. But, no matter how much Charlie trusted you, there are parts of this investigation I can't talk about."

And that's why I couldn't marry you, Al, because your principles won't allow you to trust me, or anyone.

Daniel broke in.

"I, too, have information to share, or not . . . "

I closed my notebook.

"Listen, we can each conduct our own research, or work together. I, for one, believe that if we pool our resources and information, we'll not only arm ourselves against danger, but solve this murder before someone else is killed."

We eyed each other suspiciously for a moment, then relaxed. Al spoke first.

"OK, I'll give you what I can, but no promises . . . "

At least he was willing to have a discussion. Granted, he didn't know my own reason for pushing forward.

I frowned momentarily at the memory of the black mist swirling over the canal during my frantic search for Merry. Glancing up, I found Daniel's somber eyes watching me. He cleared his throat.

"I've got some information about the bear fetish Cali found by the canal the day after the murder."

Al frowned, looking perturbed, but held his peace.

"I recognized it and the initials of the artist immediately. This bear and its twin were carved in the 1940s by a native American artisan who disappeared during the summer of 1952, while visiting Phoenix with his brother. He was known to carry the two bears with him in a small leather pouch on a lanyard around his neck."

My mind flashed back to the split-second vision of the elderly American Indian with the small bag hanging from his neck. Had I actually seen this missing artist? Why hadn't Daniel told me?

"What's this got to do with the death of Mike Sands?" I bristled at Al's brusque tone.

"Cali found the fetish by the canal, ten feet from where his body turned up. I believe either he or his murderer had the bear on his person when Sands was killed. Find the twin bear, and we may find his killer."

"And just when were you going to turn your 'evidence' over to the police?" Al's voice rose as he rounded on me. "You thought it important enough to tell him, but not me?"

Before I could respond, he turned back to Daniel.

"And what proof have you got?"

Daniel reached into his jacket and pulled a small journal with a soft, leather cover out of an inner pocket. Opening it to a yellowed page marked with a faded blue satin ribbon, he turned it towards Al and me. Illustrated in pencil and watercolor in exquisite detail, was the bear fetish, which he also pulled from the folio, still wrapped in Charlie's sock.

Unwrapping and gently setting the tiny green stone bear beside the journal, he began to turn the pages. Each page presented a delicate work of art depicting a unique animal carving, clearly dated and signed 'WST.' Most of the artwork predated 1952.

I gently pulled the journal towards me, reminded of the collection of fetishes I'd seen at the home of Tiffany and Brody Marsh.

"Well, I can't see the relevance. It seems totally unconnected to this murder." Al waved his hand dismissively, then continued.

"On the other hand, I can tell you there's no sign of Merry's leash. No one thought to look last night and there's no sign of it this morning. However, someone opened the flood control gates on the canal further up the mountain, which does explain the unexpected high level of water. The utility company denies any knowledge of it. Those gates are mostly used to regulate the flow of water off the mountain during a monsoon, but there are still one or two properties along the canal that use them to irrigate their yards."

"What I want to know, Cali, is what have you done to become a target?"

Al looked at me pointedly, and it became clear he wasn't going to contribute anything further.

I looked down at my notebook.

"Well, since Mike's death I've visited and talked to Emily and John Brennan, Tiffany Marsh, and Pat and Meghan Sands." I hesitated, then continued. "I've also been talking to Theresa Thornberg."

Al frowned. "About the case? I'd have thought Charlie taught you NOT to interfere with an on-going investigation."

I didn't answer, but I felt defensive. How dare he make assumptions about the relationship Charlie and I had? His statement sounded like a criticism of my husband, and I simply could not acknowledge it. In my heart I knew civilians like myself only made it more difficult for the police to solve crimes. Al spoke up again.

"Why all these people?"

"John Brennan is an archeologist working at ASU, and tried to start a dig on Devil's Mountain five years ago. The school shut it down without explanation. Tiffany's husband, Brody, is an architect who's done work in the past for Timmons Development, and they hired him five years ago to design a visitor's center for Devil's Mountain State Park, a project that Timmons unexpectedly pulled out of. Patricia is Mike Sand's wife, of course, and Theresa and I only went to visit her to be neighborly. But she told us that Mike had worked for Timmons five years ago as an excavator."

"Hmmm. Sounds like the common thread here is Timmons Development." Al stated the obvious conclusion, then continued.

"I wonder if Timmons Development has the power to shut down a University project? And why?" None of us answered.

"So each of these people are suspects, because someone you've spoken to set up that attempted drowning last night." I opened my mouth to mention that Mike Sands also had a green bear fetish, when Al snapped his notebook shut and stood with a growl.

"You've got to be careful, Cali. I've got more questions for you, but I don't want you leaving the house until I say it's safe!"

I glared at him.

"Just because you promised Charlie you'd look after me doesn't mean you can order me around Alfonzo Gomez! Thank you for your concern, but I can look after myself."

Al looked from Daniel to me and jammed his hat onto his head.

"Just be careful who you cozy up to." He gave Daniel one last glare, then turned and stomped out, slamming the front door.

"Oooh, he makes me so mad."

I stood for a moment staring at the front door with my fists clenched, then turned to Daniel.

"I am so sorry, he had no right to say that."

Daniel laughed.

"Don't worry, Cali . . . he's right. I do like you. You've got spirit and I suspect you're a strong woman, much stronger than you think."

He really had the softest brown eyes. Would I ever be able to have a relationship again, after Charlie? Thinking about Charlie and Daniel within the same few moments made me feel awkward and unsure of myself. But really, Daniel was here, while Charlie grew fainter and fainter.

I shook myself and looked away, uncomfortable.

"Well, I'm pretty tired after the last few days. I think I need to rest."

Daniel's smile vanished, and he became once more the serious, but sensitive, park ranger.

"Of course, call me anytime if you need anything."

He turned to leave and was opening his car door before I snapped to attention.

"Daniel, wait. Meet me for coffee at four?"

Turning slowly, he gestured towards my ankle.

"Yes, I know, but I just can't sit here waiting for something to happen."

His smile slowly crept back across his face.

"Why don't I bring dinner, and maybe a few groceries, to you instead? Your fridge is looking a bit bare."

"Um, OK, sure!" I mentally kicked myself.

I'm sure I sounded like a naive teenager. Smothering a groan, I felt old and tired.

As I closed my front door, I heard my phone ringing. Scrambling to find it before it went silent, I finally unearthed it from among the sofa cushions and punched the screen.

"Hi Cali, this is Pat Sands." There was a long pause, as if the speaker now reconsidered the wisdom of the call.

"Hi Pat, what can I do for you?" I tried to keep my voice calm, recognizing the anxiety in her voice. Pat continued in a rush.

"Theresa came into The Coffee Shoppe this morning and told Meghan who told me . . . about your awful accident in the canal last night. You were so nice to come and visit with me, I'd like to return the favor. I," she paused and started again, "I've got something I need to tell someone, and you're the only one I feel I can talk to. I can't help feeling that maybe your incident, and Mike's death must be connected somehow."

Nine

Saturday Afternoon

"I had an affair with Brody Marsh." Pat spoke softly as she carefully set her mug down on my kitchen table. She released the mug handle and pulled her hands away quickly to hide the obvious tremble, sloshing the coffee at the last minute.

Her voice shook with emotion and I was glad I'd told her to come right over. With plenty of time before Daniel would show up with dinner, I didn't really have any excuse to put her off. Exhaustion didn't count.

"I was a research librarian and met Brody about five years ago. He and Mike worked on the Devil's Mountain State Park visitor center, but then the project was cancelled, and Brody couldn't seem to let it go. He called about a year and a half ago to ask if I would research the media for Devil's Mountain . . . newspaper clippings, articles . . . stuff like that. He was still upset that Timmons had pulled out at the last minute. I never did find anything conclusive, but we . . . continued to see each other." She finally looked up. Her eyes were sad and haunted.

"When Mike died, I received this." She pulled a sheet of paper from her purse and handed it to Cali.

The note looked as though it had been printed on a printer, and contained one sentence.

I read aloud, 'Keep your hands off my man.'

Startled, Cali thought of her own note. The two weren't even remotely alike in any way.

"Did you show this to the police?"

"No. I was so ashamed of what I'd been doing, and thinking that somehow Mike had died because of . . . me, that . . . I was afraid to!" Pat began to cry.

"I know it's hard, Pat, but you really have to give this to the police."

"I guess I knew that, I've just been putting it off. Everything has been a nightmare since Mike . . . " Her words dwindled to nothing.

"Believe me, I know how hard it is to lose someone you love dearly," I had no doubt that just because Pat had acted foolishly, she still loved her husband.

"But if they are to find Mike's killer, you need to give them everything."

The thought popped into my mind that I should be doing the same . . . and hand over Charlie's shoebox to Al.

After Pat left, I returned to the kitchen, poured a second cup of coffee and grabbed my notebook. Merry wriggled in beside me as I settled into my favorite corner of the sofa and began to write out my thoughts. Most of them were questions.

The two notes were as different from each other as they could possibly be, suggesting two different writers. Mine had been hand printed block letters, and Pat's had been typed on a computer and printed from a printer. Did that mean anything?

Who would be the most upset by an affair between Brody Marsh and Pat Sands? Obviously Tiffany Marsh, or Mike Sands. But although Tiffany was a snob and the most self-absorbed person I'd ever met, she didn't seem to be a person who could commit murder. She drank too much for one thing. Remembering my visit last week I realized there might be a reason for Tiffany's self-medication. Even then something in that glass and steel palace had felt wrong.

No matter how hard I tried, I couldn't imagine Tiffany meeting Mike in the middle of, or shortly after, a monsoon, in the spiked heels and sequined dress she seemed to prefer and bashing him over the head for any reason. And why go after Mike? Why not go after Pat, since she would have been the offending partner?

None of this explained my own horrific experience in the canal, or brought me any closer to finding out who had tried to drown Merry, and possibly me. Neither I nor Merry had come to any lasting harm, so maybe it was only intended to scare me. But why? And what about the mountain spirit?

It wasn't until later that afternoon, after Pat had left, that I realized I hadn't told Al, or Daniel, about the green bear fetish Meghan Sands had said belonged to her father. So many details! I immediately sat down with my notebook and added it to the list.

How had Mike Sands found the fetish? Was it the one Merry and I found? It had to be, because otherwise it would be awfully coincidental. Was the green bear related to Brody Marsh's collection?

By the time Daniel showed up with groceries and dinner, I knew I needed to ask him about it. I hoped he'd brought the journal back with him. He'd lied when he'd taken the carved stone from me. Well, maybe he neglected to let me know he recognized it. How did I feel about his 'lying by omission?' Was it right for me to leave out important details, but not anyone else? I'd have to think about that. It did bother me a little that he'd practically threatened me with the police for not turning it in immediately.

Merry snapped to attention and bounced off the sofa just before Daniel rang the doorbell. I opened the door to find him loaded down with bags of groceries and cartons of American Chinese take-out. The scent of fried egg rolls made my mouth water as I realized I'd missed lunch.

Once all the groceries were put away, we spent a few silent moments in appreciation of sweet and sour chicken, rice, egg rolls, and white wine. I'd practically finished mine off before I remembered what I wanted to talk about.

"Daniel, why didn't you tell me at the Coffee Shoppe the other morning about your connection to the fetish?" I got the question out before he'd finished chewing, and had to wait while he leisurely completed his meal.

"I do owe you an apology." His face somber, his eyes sought mine. Looking at me almost shyly, he continued.

"I wasn't sure how much I wanted to share with you or Al about my family. I've been searching for answers for a very long time. I'm afraid I've become obsessive about it. I know I told you the fetish should go to the police, but I can't give it or the journal up. Especially after recognizing the bear."

I considered his apology for a moment, then nodded.

"OK. Can you tell me how you and the fetish are related?"

Pushing aside dishes and empty cartons Daniel carefully wiped his mouth and hands. As he reached into the inner breast pocket of his jacket to pull out the leather journal and tiny green bear, I realized he must be keeping them on his person at all times. I wondered if it was simply for security, or because he preferred to keep them as close to his heart as possible. I had so many questions I couldn't keep quiet.

"I noticed in the journal, under each illustration, the initials 'WST.' Does the 'ST' stand for Silvertree?" I pushed my own plate away and leaned on my elbows as I watched him.

Daniel looked at his hands a moment, and then smiled.

"You see so much more than most people. Do you know that?" He glanced at me and continued.

"Yes, my uncle, Wolf Silvertree, carved those animals. Those are his illustrations. This journal is his portfolio."

He lifted the cover and the small book fell open to a brittle page marked with a faded blue ribbon. The scent of dust and aging leather, and everything I loved about books, libraries, and antiques wafted across the table. It was the heady aroma of history, known and unknown, and it momentarily reminded me of the scent of the mountain spirit during my wild run down the canal. The illustration on that page, even as I leaned forward to see it upside down, looked remarkably like the stone animal sitting between us.

"Do you know what happened to his carvings?"

"No. I've been searching for him and his artwork for most of my life."

"Do you know much about your uncle's story?"

Daniel sat quietly, as if considering how much to say. Finally he looked at me and sighed.

"So much of Uncle Wolf's story is about our native American culture, and that makes it difficult to explain. The local tribal members, even though they are my mother's and grandmother's people, don't trust me. Those of us who've gone to University and have some experience living off the reservation are called 'Urban Indians."

"Uncle Wolf and my father, River, were from one of the Pueblo tribes in New Mexico. They were both proud to serve in the Army during World War II, and earned more in wages and benefits than they'd ever made on the reservation. While serving in the Army they were treated as equals by the Anglos. After the war, neither of them could get a job, or even the respect they deserved as defenders of our country.

"Uncle Wolf was the native American artisan I told you and Al about who disappeared during the summer of 1952. He and Dad left their reservation in New Mexico that year to visit Phoenix to see if they could develop a market for Uncle's artwork."

"They came to Arizona about seven years before the government started the Urban Indian Relocation Program. Phoenix wasn't one of the government-sanctioned cities. But they heard about an Anglo who lived here looking for native American art. They were only planning to be here a month. One day, Uncle left Dad in the room they'd rented, took all of his carvings and left to meet this Anglo. When he returned, he told Dad he'd exchanged the entire collection, with the exception of the two bears in the leather pouch he wore around his neck, for a piece of paper. It was the deed to a piece of land on Devil's Mountain."

Daniel shook his head and sighed.

"Dad was furious. He asked Uncle what good the paper was, if it would provide food and a roof over his head. Uncle thought it might. He didn't believe in land ownership, but things had changed drastically for our people in the last few decades. He thought maybe what the Anglo had told him was true." Daniel clenched his fists. "That Anglo was George Timmons' father, Jackson, and he told Uncle Wolf that someday the land would be worth many, many hundreds, even thousands, more dollars than it was then. Uncle Wolfe wasn't interested in large amounts of money. He just wanted a place where his children could know the earth and be free again."

I sat silent, allowing Daniel to take his time.

"The next day, Uncle left again and took the paper with him. He went to visit the mountain to see where his land was located. Timmons was supposed to meet him and show it to him personally. Wolf never returned."

"Dad searched for him and the carvings for months, then years. He settled here, met my mother and married, and had me. But he never stopped looking. He died a sad, bitter man."

"How do you think your Uncle's story is related to Mike's death?" I asked quietly.

"I don't know. But I'd be interested to see the collection you saw at the Marsh's. Are you planning to visit again?"

"I was hoping to visit Marsh next week, maybe return Tiffany's books and ask him where he got the carvings." Then I told him about my conversation with Meghan and her father's bear fetish.

"The fact that this fetish was found near the canal after Mike's death, and if his fetish missing, points to the possibility that Pat could've carried Mike's bear onto the canal just as easily as Mike himself. We really need to find the twin bear."

"Do you have any idea what happened to your Uncle?"

Daniel shook his head.

"I have my suspicions. I don't have any evidence, but I think Jackson Timmons killed Wolf, kept the carvings and the land deed, and I think his son, George Timmons, knows it."

I sat quietly, thinking over his suspicions, and came to a decision.

"Have you confronted Timmons?"

"No. As Al so clearly pointed out, I don't have any proof."

"Well, I think it's time we paid Timmons a visit. He can't sue us for asking questions."

Just as I was falling thankfully into bed my phone rang from under the pile of cushions and pillows in the great room.

As I padded out of the bedroom to search for the ringing pillow it crossed my mind that Merry could be hiding my phone on purpose.

The pillows fell silent as I found the phone next to a dog nose. Darn it, another missed call.

Punching in my numbers to hear the message, I wondered who'd be calling so late in the evening.

"Hello, Cali? This is Tiffany Marsh."

Speak of the devil. But she didn't sound like her imperial self.

"You came to visit me last week, and asked about Brody and Mike Sands, and I've found out something . . . something awful! I think I know who killed Mike Sa . . . " The message cut off abruptly.

"What . . . ?!" I waited for Tiffany to return, but the phone had gone dead.

Staring at it, I wondered what I should do. This time, I didn't hesitate before dialing Al's number. I listened to his phone ring three times before his voice mail picked up.

Where was he? One minute he's yelling at me to call him about every little thing, and now I couldn't even reach him!

After leaving a quick message letting him know I'd received an alarming voice mail from Tiffany, I called the main desk at the Phoenix Police department. Al had just been called out. Would I like to leave a message?

Phooey!

As I got ready for bed that night, my sore ankle still making dressing awkward, I couldn't shake off the words of my own note. Had someone also murdered Charlie?

And what about Tiffany? I had decided after hearing her message, and alerting the police, and trying to put my shoes on without success, that I'd done everything I physically could. It didn't relieve my feelings of guilt and anxiety. Why hadn't Al called me back?

I couldn't sleep. Rather than toss and turn, I decided to update my notes and brought my notebook to bed with me. Merry grumbled under the covers, then settled into a paw-twitching dream.

After thinking for a few minutes, I added some questions to my list.

Was Charlie murdered, and by whom?

Who has the second bear fetish?

How are the bear fetishes connected to the recent deaths?

How many murders, and murderers, are there?

At this point I paused. If Daniel's story was true, then there may be as many as three suspicious deaths: Wolf, Charlie, and Mike.

The dates of these murders divided them into three distinct time periods.

Wolf in 1952, Charlie two years ago, and Mike in the last week. Did that point to more than one killer? Most likely, and with a good possibility that all three deaths were unrelated. Ugh. The more I learned, the more complicated things became. I added another note.

Both Wolf Silvertree, and Mike Sands, had dealings with Timmons. Co-incidence?

And which death had spawned the mountain spirit? Was that even possible?

I'd forgotten to close my bedroom blinds, and as I turned off the reading lamp my eyes wandered to the window. A black smudge drifted off the hulk of Devil's Mountain and across a partial moon-lit sky. I couldn't keep my eyes open any longer, and fell asleep in the middle of a prayer for Tiffany. If something dreadful had happened to her, hers would be the fourth death.

Ten

Sunday Morning

Al called me back the following morning.

"She's what?!" I couldn't believe what I was hearing as I sat at my kitchen table. In one hand I held my phone and in the other a completely forgotten piece of cold toast. Merry sat at my feet, waiting for the toast to hit the floor.

"Dead. Sorry I didn't call you back last night, but Brody's secretary called 9-1-1 and said Tiffany jumped off her own balcony. Mentioned Mrs. Marsh was so high she probably didn't even know what she was doing." Al continued to talk but I wasn't listening. My thoughts returned to the night before, and the ominous black mist I'd seen drifting across the night sky.

Momentarily taking in Al's words, my mind spun off again. Brody had a secretary? I knew he had his office in his home. In my mind's eye I saw the flash of a white skirt disappearing around a hallway corner the day I'd paid Tiffany a visit. I'd had the distinct feeling someone had been eavesdropping that day.

The hand with the toast slowly relaxed downward, until Merry was able to reach up and gently take it with her front teeth. I didn't notice.

"We'll need to take your phone for the voice mail you received."

I didn't answer. I was trying to remember something. Something I knew was important. I snapped to attention when his latest words finally sank in.

"What? You're taking my phone?! I can't survive without my phone, Al. Can't you just come over and record the message or something? What if I have an emergency?"

For the first time I realized just how important my phone was to me. When had I become tethered to this digital lifeline?

"Maybe you could borrow your daughter's while I take yours. It'll probably only take a day to record the message and then I'd return it to you. You'd probably get it back tomorrow."

"I don't want to borrow Sophie's." That would certainly be the last straw. Any request for help from Sophie on my part and I knew I'd have to tell her everything. She'd take over my life so fast my head would spin. I tried to think of anyone else who might have an extra phone. "Let me call Theresa, maybe she and Jimmy have an extra phone."

Al showed up ten minutes later to collect my phone, and Theresa arrived just behind him with a temporary replacement.

"It's an old one of Jimmy's, but he's out working on a site. I'm sure he won't mind you borrowing it just for a day. Besides, you'll only be using it for emergencies, right? You'll just have to use our number."

I looked at it and frowned.

"You'll have to show me how to turn it on, make a call, turn it off . . . " I knew I sounded ungrateful, but really, today was just not going well.

After Al left with my phone and my temporary number, Theresa sat with me at the kitchen table, a cup of tea at her elbow, and showed me how to work the phone. It turned out to be easier than I'd thought, even though it still had the little raised, rubber buttons for numbers and not the high-tech touch screen.

"I can't believe Tiffany's dead! I ran into her yesterday morning in The Coffee Shoppe . . . she was her usually snippy self." Theresa sniffed. "Even if she was a bit of a flake, she was still one of the girls."

"I know. It just doesn't make sense. She called and left a message last night . . . it didn't sound good. If she was telling the truth, and had found out who the killer was, maybe the murderer knew that she knew. What if something happened to her . . . just as the message cut off?"

We both shuddered.

"What if he threw her off the balcony just as she called me? Maybe if I'd driven up there, or was able to reach the police sooner…"

"This isn't your fault, Cali." Theresa's voice was firm. "You did everything you could, so don't go beating yourself up over it." She paused, and then changed the subject.

"So I saw Daniel's car here last night." How could she brush off Tiffany's horrifying death so quickly? My brain was still picturing our neighbor pin wheeling into a black chasm of razor-sharp rocks.

"Um, yes, he brought dinner and groceries." I felt my face grow warm and lowered my eyes.

"Oh, come on, Cali, don't be such a prude! Tell me how it went, all the details."

I didn't really want to talk about it. I'd enjoyed my evening, but to talk about it now somehow seemed disrespectful to the woman who'd just lost her life.

"He was the perfect gentleman, we just ate and talked."

Theresa looked disappointed.

"That's it?"

"Look Theresa, I haven't been on a date since Charlie died. It was a lovely evening, but I'm going to take my time. Right now, he's a good friend. That's it."

"Well, OK. Just don't take too long, he's a good-looking guy. And you deserve to have some fun. I just want you to be happy." Theresa paused for a split second before continuing in a whisper. "You know, like me and Jimmy . . . used to be."

Theresa went quiet for a minute.

"Cali, there's something I need to tell you."

I glanced at my friend, surprised at her somber voice.

I feared she was going to tell me she and Jimmy were getting a divorce . . . or something equally as devastating.

"I've . . . been to the doctor. Oh, Cali, I've got a lump!" Theresa burst into tears.

"A lump? You mean—cancer?" I hesitated to even say the word.

I stood up immediately, hurried around the table and enveloped my friend in a tight hug.

"Oh, sweetie, I'm so sorry you have to go through this! Wait, you haven't got the results back yet?"

"Not yet . . ." Theresa hiccupped.

"Then you've got a good chance it'll come back negative. Have you told Jimmy?" Theresa nodded.

"He's panicking like it's a . . . a sure thing. He won't even talk to me about it."

"Theresa, until the diagnosis is positive, you must believe it'll come back negative. Listen, I'll come with you when you go for the results if Jimmy won't. He's just scared, like I was with Charlie."

I knew there wasn't much I could do for Theresa that would lessen her anxiety, except be there for her.

"You'll come with me?" Theresa wiped her eyes with a tissue I'd thrust into her hands.

"Of course! When is your appointment?"

"In a couple of weeks . . . and even with all that's happening around here, I just want to go home and hide!"

I sat back down in my chair and took Theresa's hand. The possibly fatal diagnosis went a long way to explain her distracted conversation.

"You know I'll be right here for you, right? Anytime you want to talk, or cry . . . or anything, I'll be here."

Theresa smiled tearfully and nodded.

"OK . . ." She whispered.

In an effort to take her mind off her problems, I spent a few minutes filling her in on some of the things Daniel and I had discovered about Mike's death. Describing the green stone bear, I told her how Merry had found it, that there were two of them, and Daniel's belief that if we could find the twin, we might find the killer. I could tell she was barely listening to me.

After another hug, Theresa left, and I returned to my kitchen table, dropping my head into my hands.

Oh, God. Not again. Please, please God, let it be a false alarm. Would bad things like this happen if Charlie were still here?

Probably. But my mind reached out anyway, looking for him, knowing he wasn't physically here, but hoping I could still feel his comforting presence.

Merry looked up at me and whined softly.

"Well, Merry, I guess I know now what's going on with Theresa and Jimmy. What an awful day!"

I fought the urge to take Merry for a vigorous walk along the canal, an activity that usually helped me get through tough days like this. My twisted ankle was a nuisance, but maybe I could sit in the shade in the backyard and draw instead. Merry loved going for walks, but enjoyed exploring every inch of her yard just as much. Our fenced-in patch of struggling grass bore the nose holes to prove it.

As I settled into the cushioned wrought iron chair and laid my pad and pencil on the glass-topped table under the covered patio, I resolved to lose myself in my drawing. Maybe while my right brain was engaged my left brain would come up with a few answers.

Several things had been tumbling around in my mind and I hadn't yet been able to tease them out. Something about Tiffany's voice mail bothered me. While my hands flew around the drawing page, my mind reviewed the words of the message. Wait, there had been something other than her words. Some other noise. As I relaxed my shoulders and concentrated on my eye-hand coordination, it finally popped into my head. Someone had been speaking in the background. I hadn't distinguished any words, but I was sure I'd heard the same voice before.

Perhaps my second visit to the Marsh estate to visit Brody, might bring me into contact with that voice. I'd have to wait until the police were done combing the home for evidence, though.

As the afternoon waned, I glanced at my pad in satisfaction. How I loved drawing. Collecting my materials I headed inside and hunted down the loner phone to call Al.

"Hi there!" I chirped when he answered.

"Hello. What do you want?" Al was always abrupt now whenever I called him, like I was going to ask him to dinner and then slap his face.

"I wondered when you'd be finished up at Tiffany's. I have some stuff of hers to return." I'd only met Brody Marsh a couple of times at public events I'd attended with Charlie, and wasn't even sure he'd recognize me. I knew I'd have to stretch the truth again, but I would return those books I'd taken from Tiffany's glass table. God was going to strike me dead one of these days for 'lying by omission.'

"Why don't I believe you? What stuff?"

"Oh, just some books." I hoped he wouldn't ask me what was in them.

Al sighed.

"I can't keep you from going up there, Cali. But please promise me that's all you're doing?"

"Really, that's what I'm doing." I crossed my fingers, choosing my words carefully.

"Well, it looks like we'll be done in two or three days. I think we'll have everything we need by then."

I knew he wouldn't elaborate so I didn't even bother to ask him what 'everything' might be.

For my next call I punched in Tiffany's cell phone number. I'd make an appointment this time, just to see who answered the phone. Not having any other phone number for the Marsh's, I was ready with my message if no one answered.

"Hello. This is the office of Brody Marsh the third, Architect."

Not expecting a human to answer, I almost dropped the borrowed phone. The same voice I'd heard in the background of Tiffany's voice mail greeted me. This must be Brody's secretary. "Um, yes, this is Cali May." I responded breathlessly. "I'm . . . a neighbor, and I borrowed a few books from Mrs. Marsh, and I'd like to make an appointment to see Mr. Marsh, return the books and offer my condolences."

"Please hold while I see if he's taking visitors."

Such a hard voice. No sounds of grief . . .I knew her job dictated she answer the phone calmly under any circumstances, but I wondered if she had even known Tiffany. She sounded . . . cold.

"Ms. May? Mr. Marsh won't be able to see you for a couple of weeks. I'm afraid he is . . . indisposed. I can put you on his calendar two weeks from this Friday."

"Oh, OK, thank you."

The line went dead.

Oh dear. Indisposed. I guessed he felt the loss of his wife keenly, despite his indiscretions.

Eleven

Monday

I awoke early the next morning with a feeling of déjà vu. Was it only a week since the violent monsoon and the horrific discovery of Mike Sands' body? And now a second body! It was still hard for me to think of Tiffany Marsh dead. Was it just coincidence? How many killers were there? And if it wasn't a coincidence, what tied the death of Mike Sands, and Tiffany Marsh together? Anything?

As I thought about Pat Sands' revelation of her affair with Brody Marsh, along with the death of Tiffany Marsh and Mike Sands, I realized Pat must be a strong contender for the number one suspect. The police might think she'd killed both her husband and Brody's wife, leaving the way open to get together with the architect.

I thought I'd better call Pat and see how she was doing. Over my eggs and toast, I pulled out my phone, and realized with a jolt that Al hadn't returned my phone yet. This was Jimmy's old phone, not mine. Oh well, it was only temporary. I quickly punched in Pat's phone number.

I immediately recognized Meghan's voice as she answered tentatively. Once I explained who I was, she burst into tears.

"Oh, Mrs. May, the police came and arrested her! They found a—a bloody tire iron in our garage; they say she hit Dad in the head with it, but I've never seen it before in my life. She loved Dad! What should I do?" Meghan wailed. I thought quickly.

"Listen Meghan, let me call a good friend of mine, an attorney. He'll take good care of your mom. And make sure you take care of yourself. Are you eating?

Meghan admitted she hadn't been and I told her to check the fridge and make a list. I hoped that would keep her busy for a few minutes.

"I'll be over in a few minutes to take you grocery shopping."

Meghan reluctantly agreed to go shopping for food with me. It would keep her occupied, I would ask her some questions, and maybe look for her father's bear fetish. For a moment I sat lost in thought.

Was Pat really a killer? Just because she'd confessed to adultery didn't make her a murderer. Why would she admit to having an affair with Brody if she had to cover up the murder of her husband?

As I pulled up outside of the Sands' home, I wondered once again if Sophie and Meghan had ever crossed paths. They seemed to be about the same age, but as different from each other as they could be. Sophie was stubborn, impulsive, often argumentative, and so sure she was always right. But she was also inquisitive. So inquisitive she'd been bored in school, and curious enough to get herself into trouble. Just like me. Meghan, on the other hand, lived completely without direction. She did whatever I told her to do without question, or interest. Even in her deepest grief, Sophie still fought her way through every day. As I remembered a particularly argumentative teenage Sophie, sitting at the dinner table arguing

with Charlie and me, for the opportunity to date a particularly nox-
ious boy. I had to smile.

Meghan came with me obediently, but her mind drifted. As we
wandered up and down the grocery aisles, I realized I would have
to make her food choices for her. I quickly took control of the cart
and began navigating for her, as she meekly followed in my wake.
We returned to her house with all the basics like bread, milk, butter,
eggs, a small box of quick rice, a few packages of frozen meals, and
a couple of things I'd been able to get her to pick out.

Whew! She focused on her own inner world to such an extent
I began to wonder if she felt up to answering any questions. She
looked exhausted and miserable.

"Meghan, is there anyone who can stay with you?"

Again it took her a few minutes to focus on the question.

"Aunt Jane, Mom's sister, lives in Apache Junction . . . "

"Listen, Meghan, do you know if your mom had any luck locating your dad's little green bear?"

She looked at me with a puzzled frown.

"I don't think so, why do you ask?" This was the first spark of
interest I'd seen out of her.

"I think it could have something to do with your father's
death."

"Will looking for it bring Mom home, or find Dad's . . . killer?"

"I don't know how or why yet, but it might."

I saw a tiny light of determination blossom behind her eyes.
Good. This might give her a task, something to do to make her
feel useful.

Why was the twin bear so important? I'd told Meghan the
truth. I didn't know, but Daniel believed there was a connection

between what was happening on the canal, the spirit, and the bear fetishes. And I wanted to believe in him.

After making sure Meghan ate at least a small sandwich with a glass of milk, I made her take a couple of ibuprofen, and put her to bed. Then I called Meghan's Aunt Jane, who agreed to drive over immediately. I also called Emily Brennan and asked her if she'd mind sitting with Meghan until her aunt arrived.

Once Emily showed up, I suffered a brief moment of guilt as I left to meet up with Daniel to plan our next steps. I could've sat with Meghan just as easily as Emily, and with a lot less hassle, but I needed Daniel's soothing aura.

My head and heart told me the killer still roamed our neighborhood.

Twelve

Monday Afternoon

Daniel drove on Monday afternoon, arriving at the corporate headquarters for Timmons Development in twenty minutes instead of the forty it would've taken me.

The building soared elegantly in the hot sun, built with the unmistakable hallmarks of Brody Marsh, with sleek lines and industrial materials. A glass-encased atrium reached into the dizzying heights above the receptionist's kidney shaped desk facing the entrance. A wall of green hothouse vines and broad leaves made a dramatic backdrop against which the desk and its single occupant stood out vibrantly.

The receptionist tapped keys on a laptop with a soft but rapid tempo, her orange fingernails flying, when a muted chime alerted her to our presence. The reception area echoed every sound, including the pleasant trickle of falling water. I hunted for its source, and finally located a thin sheet of water falling among the jungle of plants. The air felt moist and warm.

"Hello, how may I help you today?" The woman was young and as far as I could see, flawless. Not a drop of sweat anywhere. Thick red hair piled at the crown of her shapely head, and her milky white skin made a breathtaking contrast. Her perfect teeth were blinding and her apparently augmented breasts were prominently displayed in a low-cut, clinging top. As we approached, I noticed her skin-tight black leather pants and wondered which part of the corporate dress code I'd missed during my own career. Her name tag read 'Lucia.'

I wondered what she hid under the thick layers of makeup. Maybe the persona she projected came as a requirement of the job. Like the building, she appeared smooth and sleek.

"We have an appointment with Mr. Timmons. I'm Daniel Silvertree."

We'd decided I'd stay in the background as much as possible, speaking up only if I felt it necessary.

"One moment please." Lucia turned and spoke softly into her ear piece. As she swiveled to face us again, I couldn't hear a word she said as her eyes swept over each of us in turn. Her rouged lips moved as she gazed at me in speculation. What could George Timmons possibly want to know about me?

Lucia addressed us again, pointed to an elevator hidden behind the wall of plants and directed us to Timmons' office. As we approached the elevator, Daniel knelt down to tie his shoe, turned his head towards me, and lifted the index finger of his right hand to his lips for silence. Of course. Timmons could most likely see and hear us anywhere in the building.

Entering a well-appointed office of dark polished wood furniture, and marble floors covered with heirloom Navajo rugs, we were greeted by an extremely slender man with silver hair. He looked to be a well-preserved late 70s. His immaculate suit looked custom made, his shoes of the softest leather. On the hand he held out in welcome, the largest gold ring I'd ever seen caught my attention. Fascinated, I stared at the ring while Daniel greeted him. The gold had been exquisitely shaped into a serpent, which curled around his finger.

"Good morning, Mr. Silvertree. Nice to meet you Mrs. May."

He laughed at what must have been my expression of shock.

"I don't stay at the top of the real estate development industry without knowing everything I can about my visitors." Did his voice hold just a hint of a sneer? Or was that just my imagination?

"Yes, well, I'd like to ask you a few questions about your father, Jackson." Daniel didn't waste any time getting to the subject of our visit. Maybe George Timmons made his skin crawl, just as he did mine.

"Please, have a seat." Timmons waved to the two chairs in front of his desk and sat down himself. Pulling out a wooden box of cigars, he offered one to Daniel, who refused, then selected one for himself. He didn't bother to offer one to me. After leisurely cutting off the end and lighting the stogy, he finally spoke.

"What would you like to know?" His voice deceptively soft, he narrowed his ice blue eyes with heightened awareness, unblinking. His posture and attitude seemed to be channeling a slender but supple reptile. I realized he'd adapted the stance of a predator, and couldn't restrain a shiver of fear.

"Did your father ever mention a native American artist named Wolf Silvertree? He came to Phoenix after World War II in 1952. I have reason to believe they met around that time."

"Why?" Timmons snapped to attention, his voiced clipped. He placed his cigar into an ashtray on his desk, as if to have his hands free.

"In 1952 your father, Jackson Timmons, contacted him to purchase Silvertree's collection of native American fetishes. That same year both Silvertree and his collection disappeared. I wondered if either you or your father know anything about what happened to him. Is your father still alive?"

"Silvertree. He a relative of yours?" Timmons didn't bother to hide the sneer this time, but his hands were clenched so tight I could see his knuckles turning white. Without waiting for a reply, he continued.

"Why would we do business with an Indian? They were less than citizens in 1952." His tone of voice and curled lip made it obvious he believed this hadn't changed. "I very much doubt my father ever contacted, much less did business with your. . .what was he, your father?"

Daniel spoke softly. "My uncle, my father's brother. They both came here in 1952, a long way from home, with no friends, family or job. They'd been considered good enough for the U.S. Army, where they were treated with more respect than you or your father will ever know."

"If you think you're going to get a piece of my legacy on the word of a couple of out-of-work, lazy, lying bastards, then you aren't any smarter than your pa and uncle. You can just go back to the reservation where you belong. And if you come sniffing around here again, I'll sue you for slander!"

Timmons' sleek silver hair stood up straight where he'd run a hand through it during his tirade and veins in his slender neck bulged stiff and purple. We sat quietly for a moment as he pulled himself together and took a deep breath.

"I apologize. I shouldn't have said those things. My father is still alive, but he's very ill. I won't stand for any hint of scandal against him now or ever. He's a great business leader and built this backwater, wild west town into a thriving metropolis. Now if you'll excuse me, I have important work to attend to." He stood abruptly.

"Oh, and by the way Mrs. May," I froze half-way out of the chair, my breath catching at the sneer in his voice. "If you think your dearly departed husband Charlie had anything on me, my father or my company, you're gravely mistaken."

Marching us out the door, Timmons slammed it shut. As we stood, not speaking, in the hallway waiting for the elevator, I could hear Timmons' voice through the walls. He was yelling.

Daniel and I sat silent, each lost in our own thoughts as we returned to Saguaro Gulch. In unspoken agreement, he followed me into the house where Merry met us with barking, wiggles and kisses. I spent a few moments in restorative cuddles with my brave but diminutive watchdog. After washing my hands thoroughly to cleanse myself of the slime I imagined had followed us from Timmons' office, we finally settled at the kitchen table. Daniel sat across the smooth wooden surface, with glasses of ice tea and my notebook between us.

"That man is a tyrant. Evil!" I spoke in a rush.

Daniel looked thoughtful, and shook his head.

"He may sound like a monster, but we still don't have any evidence he's involved with the current murders, although his reaction seems to show he's aware something happened in 1952. I still believe; however, his father knows what happened to Wolf. If getting in to see Jackson means going through George, it may be impossible."

I could see he was worried. Watching him come this close to discovering the mystery behind his uncle's disappearance, only to be turned away at the last hurdle, broke my heart. I'd never seen him admit defeat, but as he gazed at me in raw honesty he appeared vulnerable. He'd lowered his emotional walls, inviting me in to understand the depth of his pain and frustration. When would I lower mine?

"What do you think we should do next?" His question cast a feeling of responsibility over me. He was trusting my instincts and I had to be as honest.

"I don't know." I looked down at my notebook. "Perhaps we should review my notes."

And so we did, and again we came to a dead end.

"I have the feeling the current murders are connected to your Uncle's disappearance. If you've been trying to locate him in records of the living, and not found a single hint, then he must be dead. To disappear so completely, to be here one day and gone the next, either he met with an accident, killed himself or someone took his life. Is there any reason he would take his own life, or any reason someone else would take his life?"

"All I have is Grandmother's story of his disappearance. My father refused to talk about it, although he would leave Mom and me for short periods of time when I was very young. She told me he went looking for his brother on Devil's Mountain. And then my parents were killed in a car accident, and me and Grandmother just had each other. I remember asking her as a teenager why Dad returned to the Mountain so often, and she told me his story."

As I absorbed his words, my mind wandered briefly, and I asked the question that had plagued me since the night of the monsoon.

"How does the mountain spirit fit into all this?"

Daniel looked undecided.

"Um, do you remember the sketch you made of the native American you saw when you touched the bear?" I nodded.

"I've been meaning to show you these." He reached into his breast pocket and pulled out two dog-eared, cracked, black and white photos.

"After I showed Grandmother your first drawing of the mountain spirit, she gave me these. They are photos of Uncle Wolf before he disappeared and were among the things Dad left behind when he died."

As I stared down into the face of my visions, I began to shake.

"How is this possible?"

At first glance, I immediately recognized the mountain spirit. Never having met Daniel's uncle, I gazed at the young Wolf for the first time. I couldn't miss the small bag and lanyard hanging from his neck and knew the bag contained the twin bears, both with 'WST' carved into their bellies.

"Cali, we can't know for sure that the visions you've had are of Uncle Wolf. In fact, most people would flat out disbelieve you. Even if I can prove that Timmons, or someone else, killed him, it would take a huge leap of faith on anyone's part to believe that you're actually able to see his ghost. I, however, do believe you."

He reached out and put his hands over mine until they'd stopped shaking. I had to ask.

"How do you continue to search when you've come to so many dead ends?" As the words left my mouth, I knew I needed the answer to this question. I was seeking too, I just didn't know what I needed to find. Perhaps in my heart I wanted reassurance that Charlie hadn't left me completely. He smiled.

"I believe that all of my answers will come to me, and your visions have rekindled my determination to find him. I know I will find the truth."

"You're talking about having faith, about knowing that everything will turn out right. Believing in something like the universe or God will take care of you and answer all your questions. "

"Yes."

I suddenly wanted to change the subject. I still just barely believed in my own God. Even when I'd prayed and begged, He hadn't spared Charlie.

"I can't get in to see Brody Marsh for two weeks. He apparently has a dragon of a secretary and I couldn't get past her. I wonder what would happen if I just showed up?" I pointed to the books I'd borrowed from Tiffany. "I thought I could return the books, and share my condolences without looking too suspicious. I'd like to get a photo of the fetish collection and perhaps ask Brody where they came from."

"You must be very, very careful, Cali. Have you seen the mountain spirit at all lately? You must believe in him as a warning of danger."

"N-No, well, maybe." I stuttered, and my mind flashed back to the view from my bedroom window the night before of what I had thought was smoke coming off Mountain.

Thirteen

Thursday Evening

The following Thursday evening, after a dinner of Mexican taco salad, Daniel carried two glasses of red wine into the living room.

"Do you mind if I sit next to you on the sofa?" He asked softly.

I considered for a moment. Did I want him that close?

"Um—Sure, OK." I hadn't been physically close to another human, except for momentary hugs of comfort with my girlfriends, in over two years. I didn't know how I felt about this man. I was immensely grateful he didn't laugh at my unbelievable paranormal experiences.

He sat close enough to hand me my wine, but not close enough for us to lean into each other. He smelled of fresh, early mornings after a desert rain, and radiated his usual soothing aura. After a few moments of companionable silence and a few sips of wine, he spoke.

"I received this in the mail today." He reached into his jacket and pulled out a cream-colored envelope and matching note card on heavy stock. "It's written by Jackson Timmons' lawyer, on Timmons' letterhead on behalf of his employer. Looks like Jackson signed it." He began to read.

"*Dear Mr. Silvertree,*

I have something to tell you that will help you understand the mystery in your family's past, and impact your future. Please visit me at your earliest convenience. Don't wait too long. My physician tells me I only have a week or so left before I die. You'll be doing me a favor, by allowing me the opportunity to hopefully soften my own spiritual judgment."

The bottom of the note bore the elder Timmons' spidery signature and his lawyer's contact information.

"This is good, it's exactly what you wanted, isn't it? Do you think you can trust him? When will you be going?" I had no doubt that Daniel would accept the invitation.

"I'd like to make an appointment for tomorrow, and I'd like you to come with me. I know it's soon, but I don't want to risk having him pass before I get to talk to him."

"Do you think he'll object to my being there?" I wondered if I'd be asked to wait in the car.

"Not if I tell him I won't come without you." I looked at him in astonishment.

"If we get there and he clams up because you're in the room, then I'll have you step out. But I won't have you wait in the car. You'll be just on the other side of the door. I think he has answers for me, and I want to share those with you. Will you come with me?"

"Of course!" Was he talking about the words of a dying man, or about us? I suddenly realized I wanted him to be talking about us. I wanted there to be the possibility of us. I wanted him to need me, and I wanted to allow myself to need him.

Friday Morning

On Friday morning, after a quick piece of toast and coffee for me, and a bowl of kibble and chicken broth for Merry, Daniel arrived. Merry greeted him like a long lost relative, dancing, woofing and sniffing around his feet, and finally rolling over to show her tummy for a rub. She definitely approved of him.

"Hey there, Merry. How are you and your mamma? Ready to keep the house safe while we go to work?" Merry whined and climbed onto the sofa. Somehow she knew we were going to leave without her.

"I called ahead, and Jackson doesn't have any objection to having you there." Daniel didn't look as pleased as I thought he would, and I felt a cold shiver of doubt. "It looks like it'll be George we have to worry about. He's vowed to be there with his own lawyer."

"What can he do? It wasn't his request that you visit."

"Exactly. He's saying that his father isn't in his right mind. That whatever he says might be misconstrued and used against Timmons Development. He doesn't trust us not to twist it to our advantage. So the fewer the people in the room, the better, as far as he's concerned."

"I think we should just go and see what happens." Now that arrangements were in place to visit the one person in the world that might hold the answers to the disappearance of Daniel's uncle, I didn't want any last-minute delays.

"Let's get going, then." Grabbing the backpack I'd filled with ham sandwiches, soda and chips, and several bottles of water, Daniel headed for the car.

"Sorry Merry, I know you want to come, but I don't think you'll be wanted at this meeting. I mean, they can't even agree if they want me." I gave her a hug and a scratch behind the ears, jumped up and followed Daniel out of the house.

With our appointment for 10 a.m. I was glad we'd miss the morning rush hour. The azure sky made up for the brown stretches of landscape. As we drove towards Scottsdale on the freeway the view stretched to the distant horizon in every direction. Red tile roofs, towering palm trees and lush landscaping were clustered around shopping areas to the west within the curve of highway. To the east a variety of shades of red and brown earth interspersed with green fields made a quilt that covered the valley all the way to the base of the low surrounding mountains. The vibrant colors with occasional cacti floating in the desert valley, even in the Phoenix autumn, delighted my artist's heart.

"Do you think George told his father about our visit to his office?" I asked idly as I watched stucco and concrete industrial buildings sprinkled with lush green and fiery plants fly by the car window.

"I really don't know. Doesn't make much sense though, because he's adamantly against Jackson speaking to me."

"Do you think George is really trying to protect his father, or hiding something more serious? Had your dad ever tried to contact him?"

"You know, I've been thinking about that. I don't think he did. By the time he realized Wolf wasn't returning, Dad might not have remembered Jackson's name and he certainly didn't have the deed to refer to."

"I guess we'll find out."

As we wound our way through Paradise Valley, we came to an upscale, gated community of sprawling homes. Daniel punched in the code Jackson's attorney had given him, and we drove through the gate as it silently slid to one side.

The elder Timmons' home was Spanish in style, stuccoed white with red roofing tiles. Every inch of earth around the stately home appeared landscaped with gravel, grass, lush palms and cobbled walkways. I wondered how much money Jackson Timmons had accumulated over his long life.

The circular drive already had three cars parked on it. Daniel pulled his Jeep in behind a Lexus, BMW, and Cadillac SUV, and we climbed out just as the front door opened. George Timmons stood in the doorway with his arms crossed.

"Hello, George. Beautiful day, isn't it?" Daniel greeted him.

George shot both of us cold nasty looks, pursing his lips as he reluctantly moved aside to let us in.

"If I had my way, you wouldn't be here. However, my father has threatened to have me thrown out of his will and the meeting, if I object too strenuously. And God knows, I want to hear what he's got to say."

We followed him down a cool hallway paved with terra-cotta tiles. He led the way into a large bedroom with wide windows displaying sweeping views of the back acreage. His father, Jackson, lay propped against several pillows in a bed made from whole tree trunks. It was a rustic, southwest masculine room with few knick-knacks.

"I'm glad you came. I'm so pleased to meet you, Mr. Silvertree, Mrs. May." The old man's voice sounded weak and gravelly.

"If you'll all take seats, I want to get started right way. No telling how much time I've got." He drew a deep, wet breath, coughing the phlegm into a cotton handkerchief.

He then pointed to Daniel.

"Would you please show your identification to my attorney here? Landon, please confirm it." The man standing on one side of the bed stepped forward, and held out his hand for Daniel's drivers' license.

"I'm already pretty sure you are the son of River Silvertree, nephew to Wolf, and the next surviving kin of each. But it never hurts to double-check."

"Dad—I don't really think this is—"

"I don't care what you think, George. I'm not doing this to save my reputation. I'm doing this to save my soul, and yours." I barely caught the last words as he ran out of breath.

The old man cleared his throat once more, and started talking.

"In the spring of 1952, someone brought me a native American fetish. At the time I was attempting to develop a market for Native American art in Phoenix. It was one way to attract tourists to this God-forsaken place. It was a dust bowl then, not what you see today.

"It was exquisite. The fetish, I mean. So I wrote a letter to the artist. It was one thing to deal in priceless, handmade art, quite another to deal with the artists who created it. No disrespect intended, but your father and uncle were Indians. With that label came all of the preconceived sins the Anglos laid at the feet of our country's original inhabitants. I wasn't any different.

"Wolf brought me the most amazing collection of animal carvings I'd ever seen, and I wanted them. Used to getting what I wanted back then, I knew I could get them for practically nothing. I came up with a way to seem to pay for these priceless artifacts, knowing your uncle had no idea of their worth."

Jackson relaxed back on his pillows and took several breaths. His lawyer helped him take a few sips of water.

"I'm not proud of what I did. I had the devil in me and he sang as sweet a song as any I've ever heard."

"Oh, come on, Dad! What could you have possibly done -"

"Shut up, son!" George slouched back down in his chair with an expression of confusion and hurt in his eyes.

"I convinced him to sell them to me in exchange for a piece of property up on Devil's Mountain. This was before the government stepped in and turned most of it into a state park. Luckily I still own that piece."

"I offered to take him up the mountain to see the actual parcel." Again Jackson went quiet.

Daniel sat, not moving. I was watching his eyes as we listened to the old man's narrative. Having already theorized the same events, I wondered how Daniel was dealing with the fact that he'd been right.

"I—I showed him around a bit, and he seemed to appreciate the property in ways I couldn't begin to understand. I hadn't gone to meet him with the intention of killing him." Tears began to slide silently down his face. "I didn't think I was a bad person, just greedy. It was too easy. I knew I could have both the art collection, and the land."

"He faced away from me, looking out over the valley, and I picked up a rock, and hit him on the back of the head." His voice shook. "I've regretted it ever since. It haunts my dreams, I've felt him watching me from the shadows in this very room at night." Jackson was whispering now. The rest of us sat or stood in various states of shock. Even though I had expected an unsettling story, the emotions triggered by the truth threatened to overwhelm me. I felt my eyes burning with unshed tears.

George sat in his chair in the corner, his hands over his face. The two lawyers stood awkwardly by the bed. One held a tape recorder. Jackson roused once more.

"You get that on tape?" He nodded to his man, who replied, "Yes, Sir."

"Well I'm not done." One more deep breath.

"That deed is with my lawyer along with a letter I wrote. When George told me yesterday that you'd come to him asking questions, I knew I had to speak up. I didn't make the decision to make things right overnight, you know. Quite a while ago I wrote instructions into my will, leaving that piece of property to you, Mr. Silvertree. If I could return the fetish collection to you as well, I would, but I'm afraid my son—misplaced it."

Daniel cleared his throat.

"Mr. Timmons, why didn't you contact my father before me? Why did you wait this long? He spent his whole life looking for his brother."

In the heavy silence that filled the room I felt sure Jackson had said his piece.

"I didn't fear death enough to make things right with your father. I wasn't a nice man." Jackson whispered with his eyes closed. A slight smile lifted the corners of his mouth.

"I hope You'll forgive me—" He finished, and fell silent. I had no doubt he wasn't addressing any of the humans in the room.

Fourteen

Monday Morning

Less than 24 hours after our visit with the old man, Jackson Timmons died in his sleep. Daniel received an invitation to attend the reading of the will, scheduled to take place the following week. We both anticipated a bitter legal battle over the ownership of the parcel of land on Devil's Mountain.

In the meantime, the police were called in and given the recording of Jackson's confession. I wanted to ask Al how his investigations were going, but he studiously avoided me. A few days later Daniel called me.

"The authorities have located Uncle Wolf's - remains - and wanted to know if I would like to see them. Want to come along?"

"Um, viewing human remains isn't my favorite date, but I'll come with you if you want me to."

My attempt at humor fell flat, as Daniel continued in a serious tone.

"You are very sensitive to small details, and I'd like to know your thoughts after we've seen the bones. I can stop by and pick you up just after lunch." This had to be the strangest invitation I'd ever had, but how could I refuse? I chalked it up to morbid curiosity.

We agreed he'd pick me up on his way to the Phoenix morgue. I tried not to eat too much for lunch, not being sure how my stomach might react to the look and smell of death. Reaching Jefferson

Street in downtown Phoenix, we parked as I tried not to think about what awaited us.

"How do they know it's your uncle?" I figured I couldn't even pretend to know how these things worked.

"Right now, it's only on the word of Jackson Timmons that the authorities suspect the remains might belong to my uncle. I imagine I'll have to provide DNA eventually to confirm it. I'm hoping I can get Uncle Wolf back into the earth soon with a proper burial ceremony." I knew he wasn't referring to an Anglo funeral.

Our footsteps echoed as he led me down a corridor, shiny with sterile white walls and floors. An attendant met us at an intersection and we followed him the rest of the way into a small room with a metal table covered with a white sheet. The cloth was oddly lumpy, and I wasn't surprised as it was folded gently back to reveal a collection of long bones, bits and pieces of toes and fingers, and a skull. There were also knots of hair and torn, discolored fabric. The attendant asked us not to touch anything, but gave us permission to visually examine and photograph the remains.

I felt a bit squeamish as I stared at the yellowish skull, trying to picture it behind a human face, a face loved by his family, his friends and especially his brother, River. In an effort not to embarrass myself by losing my lunch onto the pristine floor, I started examining the tiniest of details. Pulling out a small sketchpad and pencil, I started with the skull. Drawing the jaw line and working my way up the side of the forehead, my pencil outlined every crack, rough patch, and misalignment. Concentrating on the smallest shapes first allowed me to sketch the whole collection without thinking about it as the structural support inside of what used to be a living, breathing human being.

I wondered if it would be easier if I knew nothing about the individual it belonged to. Knowing even the small amount of information that I now knew from Daniel about his uncle made the exercise horrifying. Finally finished, I looked down at the pad and realized I'd sketched the only pieces left of Wolf Silvertree. Daniel stood with his head bowed and I felt an overwhelming sadness that he never knew this talented relative.

"I'm done." His voice came out in rough whisper, and the attendant covered the remains again. We made our way out of the bowels of the building, found our car and drove to my house in silence.

"I won't be coming in, Cali. I need to return to Grandmother and show her the photos I took." I hadn't even been aware of the photo flashes in my preoccupation as I sketched.

"Call me if anything occurs to you, and I'll be by tomorrow. Thank you for coming with me." We briefly made eye contact before I climbed out of his Jeep.

Meeting me at the door, Merry's joyous greeting lifted me out of my sadness.

"Oh, Merry. I've never really thought about what parts of us get left behind. It's such a difficult task to look at a collection of bones and know they were once a person. But they are all that's left of a living, breathing, feeling human, with a family. How fragile we are!"

With that I settled onto the sofa with a hot sugary cup of tea and my sketchbook. Pulling Merry in close beside me, I reviewed my drawings. Trying to be objective, I allowed my eyes to follow the pencil lines once more, avoiding the gaping eye sockets and exposed teeth, and the crush of broken bone showing through from the back of the skull. On the side of the forehead I found an interesting shape. I couldn't remember if or where I'd seen it before, but it seemed an unusual zig-zag imprint with a triangular shape at one end.

Finally I gave up.

"Ready for a walk, little girl?" Merry bounced and wiggled her agreement.

Tuesday

When Daniel returned the next day I showed him my drawings, and though we poured over them for a couple of hours, we could not come up with anything insightful.

Al showed up and spent more hours than I would've liked in my living room going over details of the murders. He alternated between scolding me for doing such 'damn foolish things' like talking to my neighbors, and then telling me how he solved the murders and apprehended the murderer, Patricia Sands.

"We're building a case against her, so don't you go messing things up by trying to find someone else for a suspect."

Just one more reason why he and I would not have been a good thing.

"Al, Charlie never forced the evidence to fit the theory. You can't convince me that Patricia killed Mike and Tiffany. There has to be someone else. I just don't know who it is yet. I want you to leave me alone, I need space to think! Framing Patricia doesn't answer the question of the two different notes, or trying to drown Merry in the canal, for a start."

Al looked at me, first hurt, then angry.

"Well, then, you just keep yourself out of trouble, do you hear me? I don't want to be rescuing you again."

"Look, Al, it's not that I'm not grateful or don't like visiting with you, but we've really talked these murders to death, and unless you're going to take the fetish I found and my threatening note about Charlie seriously, then I think we're done."

"Those things were never really a part of Mike Sands' death. If you find out anything that might connect them, then give me a call. And by the way, this is my investigation, and I decide when it's done."

He stomped out of my house and drove away.

I knew he still hurt but he drove me crazy, especially when he always had to be right.

Wednesday Morning

Daniel picked me up at 9 a.m. on Wednesday morning to attend the reading of Jackson Timmons' will, at the office of William Landon, Timmons' lawyer. It was scheduled for 10 a.m. in downtown Phoenix.

You would have thought someone as rich as Timmons would have either paid his lawyer enough for a larger office, or chosen a lawyer with an office large enough to fit more than twelve chairs, shoulder to shoulder in front of his desk. As people quietly shuffled in and sat, I began to sweat as the temperature in the tiny room began to soar.

Once all the chairs were full, I found I didn't recognize anyone but George Timmons. He arrived late. The proceedings couldn't start without him, which I suspected he knew. Before taking the last seat reserved for him at the front, his ice blue eyes swept over the rest of us, and landed with a sneering squint on Daniel.

"Please take your seat, Mr. Timmons, and we'll get started." The lawyer mopped the moisture off his brow with a handkerchief from his breast pocket. Several large ladies were fanning themselves with assorted scraps of paper. I could feel a trickle of sweat making its way from my hairline, down my neck, and down between my breasts. Afraid to look down to see if the perspiration appeared in wet patches on the front of my short sleeved, silk blouse for fear of attracting unwanted attention, I struggled to ignore it.

Most of the bequests were modest amounts of money to loyal employees. After almost an hour, the lawyer paused. He hadn't yet mentioned either George, or Daniel.

"We now come to a most unusual bequest. It was added recently and includes a letter from Mr. Jackson Timmons." Clearing his throat, he began to read.

"To my son, George, I leave my four homes, and a small stipend for managing them and paying the property taxes. I also leave him my collection of vintage automobiles and the garage to keep them in. I leave him everything remaining, with one exception."

"The parcel of land as described below, on Devil's Mountain, I leave to Daniel Silvertree, in recognition for the profound trauma my family has caused his. Both Daniel, and George, are aware of the details. I've included a small amount of cash, in the amount of $150,000 to pay any taxes on the property and other needs. The letter accompanying this document explains the circumstances of this bequest."

As if waiting for an impending explosion, the tiny room dripped sweat from various overheated guests as they held their collective breath. No one moved, and after 30 seconds, it came.

"I won't stand for this! If you think for one minute I'm going to let him get away with this -- this travesty, not to mention the fact that my father was obviously out of his mind when he confessed --" George suddenly seemed to remember he was in the company of many who had no idea of Jackson's confession and awkwardly swallowed his next words.

The lawyer continued.

"There is one last sentence."

"My son George may not remember everything as it happened in 1952 concerning the death of Wolf Silvertree, and it would be of great benefit to him to not dig too deeply for alternative answers."

This time, everyone stared at the man behind the desk. With no further explanation, he finished.

"The reading of this will is complete. You will all be receiving a letter explaining what to expect as these bequests are fulfilled. Thank you." With that, he left the room.

A murmuring of low but excited conversation broke out among the attendees as they stood and slowly trickled out of the office. Daniel and I were the last to enter the hallway. We were heading for the stairs, when a voice reached out to us.

"I have no idea what my father is referring to, and it doesn't matter. You will not be getting any land or money. I will be contesting the will." George Timmons swept past us and moved down the stairs, once more the supremely self-confident, exquisitely polished businessman, with the sun from a window in the stairwell glinting off his silver-white hair and the gold ring I'd noticed on his hand the first time we'd met. He appeared so cool, I entertained the idea that he must be superhuman not to be covered in a sheen of perspiration like the rest of us.

Daniel offered me his arm as we quietly left the building, both of us thoughtful.

"What do you suppose Jackson meant in that last sentence?" I looked across the tiny, round cafe table at Daniel. We'd stopped for refreshment at the Coffee Shoppe after the will reading, waving to Meghan as we ordered and then carried our drinks and Danish to a corner table.

"I'm not sure. I wonder how old George was in 1952? Jackson lived to be 98."

We both sat frowning at the effort to mentally calculate George's possible age.

"If his father was 34 in 1952, George couldn't have been much older than 12 or 13 years old. How could a child of that age be involved in a murder?"

Fifteen

Thursday Morning

I should have felt a sense of relief now that the murders of Mike, Tiffany and Wolf had been solved. But things still didn't add up. Who had tried to drown Merry, and left the threatening note behind? The writer had hinted that my dear Charlie hadn't died on his own. How could that have been possible? None of his physicians had even questioned his death from cancer.

The day after Jackson Timmons' will had been disclosed, Daniel, Merry and I walked along the canal. I'd been whining about feeling dissatisfied with our investigation when Daniel interrupted me.

"I agree."

I stumbled over a clod of dirt in surprise.

"You do? I thought I was just being moody, blowing off steam."

"But you do have unanswered questions, and I have a few of my own. For instance, what were those strange statements Jackson mentioned on his deathbed? Why would he be confessing to save his soul, and to somehow benefit George, other than with money and land? Why would he warn George off investigating Wolf's murder?"

In my self-absorption I had completely forgotten those details. And as I reviewed the reading of the will, I again saw, in my mind, the flash of sunlight as George swept down the stairs ahead of us.

"Maybe we should go back to my notes." I was sure I hadn't made any new comments since the police had arrested Patricia, but it couldn't hurt.

Daniel nodded, pre-occupied with his own thoughts and we turned around and headed back towards my house.

As we approached, Merry started barking up a storm. An unfamiliar black BMW with dark-tinted windows sat in my driveway. The doors opened, and two men climbed out, both with dark glasses and black clothing. Who were they? Secret agents?

As they removed their glasses I recognized George Timmons and his attorney, William Landon. George looked awful, with dark pouches under his eyes and new lines on his face. Just as I was about to greet him, a police car with its sirens screaming and lights flashing drove up and screeched to a halt. Al pulled his bulk from behind the wheel and scowled at me, then swiveled to confront George.

"Mr. George Timmons?" He barked.

Timmons turned to look at him, his face creased in mild surprise.

"What do you want?"

"I'm here to arrest you for the murder of Wolf Silvertree."

Everyone froze, like a dramatic tableau in a painting.

"What are you going on about, Al?" I broke the silence and stuck my face in his.

"Now, Cali, you stay out of this."

"Why don't we all go inside and sit down with some nice glasses of iced tea?"

"Cali, you don't understand..." Al sputtered.

"Well, maybe you can explain it to us." And with that I marched up to my front door and invited everyone inside. I really didn't want Al making a scene outside in front of all my neighbors.

Once we were all settled, some more awkward than others, in the living room, each with a glass of iced tea, I turned to Al.

"Now, go ahead, Al. Tell us why you're arresting George."

"Well, I gotta ask him some questions first." He admitted, nodding to George and starting at once.

"Mr. Timmons, where'd you get that ring?"

"My. . . father gave it to me." George looked bewildered.

"How long have you had it?"

"Uh, all my life. He gave it to me when I turned 13. Why? What's it got to do with anything?"

"Well, the coroner did a preliminary on the bones we recovered from that plot of land that your father gave to Mr. Silvertree here." Al frowned at Daniel, then continued.

"There's a mark on the side of the skull that's not natural. How old were you in 1952?"

Suddenly I knew what Al was going to say. I quietly stood and grabbed my drawing pad, and flipped to my sketch of the skull. The unnatural zig-zag with the triangle at one end seemed to match the gold snake ring George now twisted nervously around his finger.

"I—I was 14. But I don't—I mean, I didn't know anything about what Dad—confessed." George swallowed nervously, blinking several times.

"Well, you may not remember it, but that imprint on the side of the skull looks like it was made with your ring." We all looked as George held out his hand, and stared at the gold snake wound around his finger. His hand started to shake, and his eyes glazed over, as if trying to remember something awful.

"But I don't—I can't remember..." He whispered. I began to realize that if he had anything at all to do with Wolf's death as a child, he might have wiped it from his memory out of the sheer horror of it.

"Al, how can you be sure George wore the ring that day? Jackson could've borrowed it and a child that young might not even have known it." I suddenly felt Charlie standing right behind me and I knew he agreed. With Jackson, and all of Wolf's generation dead, what good would it do to stir it all up again? Daniel, of course would need to press charges, but what if he didn't?

Daniel watched George thoughtfully, who by this time was shaking visibly. Daniel addressed him.

"What are you doing here, at Cali's house?"

"I—I wanted to have my attorney serve you papers, to sue you for the return of my property. We called your office and finally tracked you down here."

No one spoke for a minute. I had the feeling no one, not the attorney, or the policeman, knew what to do. Suddenly I spoke. Maybe Charlie prompted me.

"You know, no one really knows what happened except for what your father told us. Why don't you rip up those court papers, and Daniel here won't push the authorities to prove you might have been involved in a murder." I knew it couldn't be proven but George looked so sick I thought he might pass out. I looked over at Daniel to see if he approved, and he winked.

Al cleared his throat and gave me a half-smile. His expression confused me, because the Al I knew would've broken into a lecture about letting the police do their job. Maybe Al wasn't as bull headed as I thought. He spoke up sheepishly.

"Cali's right. I followed Mr. Timmons here on the off-chance he'd confess if I confronted him with the evidence. But we don't need to pursue it. We've already got a taped confession." He paused for a moment, as I sat with my mouth open.

"Guess I might as well be going." Al shifted his bulk, stood up and even gave Merry a pat on the head. He gently but firmly closed the front door behind him as I watched him leave, overcome with astonishment. When had Al become so sensitive?

"I—I really don't remember, I don't want to remember!" George blurted out. His lawyer leaned over and whispered in his ear, and George turned even whiter.

"Listen, you keep the property and the cash my father gave you. It's yours. I don't want anything to do with it! And . . . and about your uncle's fetish collection . . . I gave it to Brody Marsh, in return for the design of the visitor's center. I couldn't find the deed to the property, couldn't prove the land was mine, so I had to cancel the project. I didn't have the funds to pay him and didn't know the collection wasn't mine and—oh God, I think I need help!"

As Daniel and I watched the lawyer help his client into their car, I saw George frantically trying to tug the ring from his finger, without success.

That night as Merry and I sat by ourselves, snuggled on the sofa, I returned to my last few questions. With my notebook open, as well as my drawing pad, I reviewed the night Merry had been mysteriously caught in the rushing water behind my house. How had she gotten over, or through, the fence? With her leash? Someone had to have put her leash on her and then fastened it to the grate. I didn't think Al believed me when I'd told him about that.

I tried to remember what I'd been aware of as I'd limped down the canal. Merry's crying, certainly, but what else? Something about a firefly. But we don't have fireflies in the desert. Could it have been a cigarette? And how did whoever it was get into my house in the first place? There weren't that many people who had a key. I'd lent one to Theresa once when Charlie and I went on vacation, but she'd given it back. My daughter Sophie had a key, which I kept meaning to get back but kept forgetting to ask for. The only other person who had one was Daniel. I'd finally given him one just a couple of weeks ago, because he came over so often that Merry was driving me nuts with her barking every time he knocked. Maybe Charlie had given our key to someone. Al, maybe? What if it was someone I didn't even know?

Finally I scooped Merry into my arms and headed for the bedroom. Merry was half asleep and didn't stir as I lay her on the bed. I kept the bedside light on, let Merry snuggle into a comfortable sleeping position, and prepared myself for a sleepless night. I was petrified. What horrors would there be if I fell asleep? Would my dreams be interrupted by visits from various ghosts? But no matter how much I didn't want to close my eyes, I couldn't keep them open.

"Cali."

Awaking in a sweat, I heard the echo of my name. Terrified at what might be in the room with me, I lay frozen, straining to hear. Merry shifted in her sleep, bringing me a moment of reassurance, and I opened my eyes slowly. Someone stood at the foot of my bed. Oh God! Maybe I really was insane.

As I watched the figure shimmer in and out of the shadows, I began to feel angry.

"Are you Wolf Silvertree?" The words, meant to sound confident and commanding, came out in a breathy squeak. There was no response, as if sensing my anger.

But I knew who, and what it was. The mountain spirit had come alone, without Charlie, and stood before me. Once more he held out his hand. It was empty this time, and he didn't bother to speak, but I could see more detail than before. Although he held his head high, his eyes and mouth turned downward, and he slowly lowered his hand. Such a wave of sadness washed over me I could feel my eyes blur with tears, as he slowly faded away. I was sure this was Daniel's Uncle Wolf.

I lay awake for the rest of the night. Not from fear, but from anger. By the time I dragged myself out of bed the next morning, I wanted to scream. The bed clothes were damp with sweat, and Merry lay gazing at me from the other side of the bed, having moved as far away from me during the night as she could without getting off. Apparently I'd been too restless.

As I made my way to the kitchen, my jaw hurt from grinding my teeth. I had to solve the mystery behind the mountain spirit before it drove me crazy. During the night I had finally admitted to myself that I could see ghosts, and there had to be a darn good reason for this unsettling ability. If I couldn't figure out why I was being haunted, the spirit might never leave me alone.

Sixteen

Friday, 3:00 P.M.

On the day of my appointment with Brody Marsh, he opened his own front door.

"Yes?" He squinted at me from the dark interior, eyes red-rimmed.

"Oh, hi, I, um, I have an appointment to see you at 3:00. My name is Cali May and I am, was . . . a friend of Tiffany's. I'm so sorry for your loss."

I stood there, awkward and uncomfortable.

"I'd like to return some books she lent me…"

My words faded as I saw the confusion in his face.

"Brody, who is it?" I started at the voice behind the door. It was the voice in the background of Tiffany's voice mail. Who was this?

The door opened wider as the speaker confronted me and smiled.

"Oh, yes, hi Cali." Turning to Brody, the woman shooed him into the recesses of the house. "You just go rest, Brody, and I'll take care of this. Cali doesn't need to see you."

Cali watched as Brody shook his head as if to clear it. He slowly turned and stumbled down a marble paved hallway.

"Poor thing, he's devastated." the woman turned back to me, waved me in and closed and bolted the door.

I stared at her in amazement. It couldn't be. Before me, with her chin raised, her mouth in a sneer and fists on hips, stood Peggy Jo Baker. The very same Peggy Jo I'd seen as the mousy treasurer at the WODM meeting. Only this Peggy Jo was supremely self-confidant. Her hair was a thick, shiny blond, and her shoulders were back, her chin up. She was dressed exquisitely in a dress I could have sworn I'd seen Tiffany wear once. And she'd just locked the front door.

"Peggy Jo, I didn't expect to see you here." I blurted out.

"No, I don't suppose you did. You didn't think little old me could possibly get such a plumb job with the most handsome, and now eligible man in town, did you?" Peggy Jo's mouth twisted into a grin.

What was she talking about?

Peggy Jo led me into the bowels of the enormous house, entered an office the size of a walk-in closet and waved to a chair. Then she sat behind the modern, sleek-lined desk. A shelving unit stood against one wall, with several monitors mounted on the wall above it. They showed several views of the house and I decided they were security cameras. The shelves were loaded with books, and on the top shelf rested a terrarium with what looked like a variety of toads and lizards. Next to it bloomed a tall, tropical plant with shiny green leaves and fleshy purple blossoms. The flowers stood out against the all-white walls. I noticed the floor was still uncarpeted marble, and the chair I sat on was on wheels.

"Have a seat, Cali, while I call for tea."

Said the spider to the fly, I thought to myself.

As Peggy Jo clapped, very much like Tiffany had on her last visit, I slid my hand into the pocket of my jeans. I knew I'd only have seconds before Peggy Jo noticed what I was doing.

As Peggy Jo cleared the desktop of papers, a soft whisper of fabric sounded outside the open door. The maid I remembered from my last visit stood in the hallway with a tray loaded down with a teapot, cups, sugar and creamer, and a plate of cookies. I tried to remember her name. Rosa?

"Just set it on the table in the hall, I'll get it in a minute." Peggy Jo commanded.

Rosa shot me a quick glance and gave her head an almost imperceptible shake, then lowered her eyes, set the tray on the side table by the door in the hallway and disappeared.

"Such a hard worker, Rosa." Peggy remarked. "Too bad she doesn't speak English. She couldn't call for help if her life, or anyone else's, depended on it."

She stood, stepped into the hallway and collected the tray. Out of sight for only a moment, she reappeared and set the tray on her desk.

"Now where was I?"

Peggy Jo continued to talk as she poured two cups of tea, and offered me the sugar and creamer.

"Oh, yes, Tiffany Marsh and Mike Sands. Tiffany, bless her little heart, felt sorry for me. Can you imagine that? And when she and Brody decided he needed a part-time secretary, she offered me the position. She thought she was doing me a favor, wanted me to scrape and bow to her as mistress of the house. Well, I knew why I'd been placed in this home. God wanted me to save Brody from all the back stabbers and leaches in his life. When I fell in love with him, I knew right away that he loved me just as much, and I knew my job was to get rid of anyone who could hurt him."

"But I don't understand, Peggy Jo. Why would anyone want to hurt Brody?"

I knew I sounded weak, but I had to keep Peggy Jo talking and hoped something happened that would allow me to escape. I took a tiny sip of my tea. Maybe if I acted predictably and stayed calm, Peggy Jo would come to her senses.

"Oh, I expected much more than that from you, Cali. After all, you are the wife of a police detective. You don't care about Brody! And you don't even know me, you have no idea how I've struggled through life, with everyone writing me off as a small insignificant sort of person."

Cali felt the sip of tea hit her stomach and begin to burn.

Oh my God, was Peggy Jo completely psycho?

"Did -- did you kill Tiffany? Or Mike, or even Charlie? Did you try to drown my dog?" I knew I was losing my cool, but I felt nauseous and dizzy. I looked over at the terrarium toads and the plant, and back at my teacup.

"Of course I didn't hurt your poor little puppy, why would I do that? I love animals. It's people I can't stand. And if I remember correctly, your precious hubby died a slow and agonizing death from cancer."

Peggy Jo smiled slowly, with a hint of a snarl.

In that moment, I hated the person sitting in front of me. A hopeless frustration, mixed with grief momentarily blinded me as my body began to convulse.

Peggy Jo laughed softly.

"You're not afraid of little old me, now, are you? I'm damaged goods, you know. My father beat me, and my mother, tired of her own beatings, left us. She abandoned her only, small, insignificant daughter and left me with a mad man. But I survived, I killed him before he could kill me. And I've been fighting ever since. Society owes me. Oh sure, the neighbors knew what he was doing, but did they say anything, do anything? No. I was completely alone. A six-year-old against a brutal maniac. No one cared."

I was very afraid of Peggy Jo Baker, who had become Jekyll and Hyde incarnate, but I was determined to get some answers.

"But why Mike?" My stomach rolled and clenched painfully.

My hostess let out an ugly laugh.

"Patricia Sands thought she could get away with her little tryst with Brody, but I knew all about it. She had to be punished, and what better punishment than to take away her own love, the man she was supposed to be loving? And it was a great move on my part, because when I got rid of Tiffany, the sniveling bitch, all the suspicion, for both deaths, fell squarely on Pat."

"How's that?" I struggled to breathe.

"I met with Mike on the canal, and crushed his tiny brain with a tire iron. I planted it in Pat's garage. Mike thought I was going to buy that stupid little bear for Brody's collection. Instead I told him something about his wife's occasional 'night's out with the girls.' He was so dumb, he didn't believe me. He told me I was nuts. And he was angry! Imagine that -- angry at me for calling him out in the middle of a monsoon! It wasn't my fault his wife was playing around, or that he wanted to unload stolen art, or that the weather decided at the last minute to explode. He turned his back on me to leave, and I hit him and rolled him into the canal."

Peggy Jo grinned triumphantly. She clearly expected me to congratulate her, but by now I was listening with only half my mind. The other half was frantically trying to figure out what I should do. Once again, my curiosity had gotten me into trouble. Getting a closer look at Brody's fetish collection seemed irrelevant now.

I began to feel like I'd been planted in wet cement. My limbs refused to obey my mind.

"Then you had to point the police in my direction. You suggested I had mugged myself and stole the WODM money, and damn, stupid old Al Gomez believed you! He came up here all puffed up with his own importance with a search warrant. Luckily I'd already hidden the money elsewhere. It's my get-away money. And I suspect the Women of Devil's Mountain won't be thrilled when they find out I didn't even open a bank account for them."

I was in too much pain to express my surprise at Al's taking my angry outburst seriously or even the fact that the WODM treasurer had never intended to open a bank account, or manage and deposit their money.

Peggy Jo stood, and calmly pulled a roll of duct tape and a pair of gloves from her top drawer.

"You think you're so smart. I added a little something to your cup out in the hallway. If you'd finished drinking it all up like a good girl, you'd be dead by now. But I can work with you this way just as easily."

Damn. I hadn't thought—and I couldn't think now.

Once she had the gloves on, she advanced and quickly taped my arms and legs to the chair. Then she wheeled me out of the office and down the dark hallway.

As we entered a room I'd never seen, I realized we were in another of the many steel, marble and glass social spaces that hung off the mountain into thin air. Peggy Jo wheeled me towards the glass wall that looked out over the Valley, slid two glass panels aside and pushed the chair ahead of her out onto a balcony. Two smooth white leather chairs with a small Plexiglas cube for a table between them were elegantly arranged just within my circle of vision. A five-foot, glass, see-through barrier, rose between us and the drop into the deep ravine below.

I could hear and see everything. I just couldn't move. My body felt numb. I couldn't feel my tongue. The paralysis was almost complete. If the intense pain in my stomach caused me to vomit I'd choke to death. Where were Rosa and Brody? Were they just going to let this mad woman kill off people one by one? Were they going to let me die? Or were they dead already?

"Oh, and by the way, you don't have worry about Brody. He's upstairs sleeping off a nice relaxing medication I gave him to help him deal with his grief. Once I get him to sign over his bank accounts, I think I'll take a little vacation, maybe take him with me. Of course, he may not love me so much now, but I can deal with that."

"Now, Cali, I'm going to wheel you over to the balcony wall here and remove the tape. Once I tip you off the balcony, your body will be well hidden in one of the deepest ravines on this bloody mountain where no one will ever find you. I stupidly threw Tiffany off one of the other balconies where they were able to spot her. And even if they do find you, they won't find any trace of the poison in your body. Tiffany did most of my work for me, of course, with all her prescription meds. She was so totally out of it she had no idea what was going on when I tipped her over the edge."

I could hear the tape being ripped away from my arms and legs, but couldn't move my head to see. Peggy Jo was grunting with effort but seemed to be maniacally strong enough to lift me out of the chair, which rolled away as I was pulled vertical.

Random thoughts raced, disjointed, through my head. This couldn't be happening. She couldn't possibly be strong enough to lift my body over the wall.

Peggy Jo raised my arms above my head and leaned my body against the wall. All she needed to do was maneuver my center of gravity up onto the edge of the glass barrier and then tip my legs up.

My arms now hung out over the ravine below and I tried to relax my body into a dead weight, hoping it would make Peggy Jo's job that much harder. Once my waist reached the top of the wall, I knew I was dead.

As I hung helplessly over the ravine, my muscles began to convulse. My breath came in short choppy breaths as my lungs began to fight for air.

Again, my mind went its own way. What was I doing here? I was going to die in this place and time, and for what? I couldn't remember.

Shouting, loud noises, screaming, and several hands reached for me all at once. Al swam into focus, and then Daniel, along with other faces I couldn't identify. An overwhelming feeling of relief washed over me along with intense nausea as I finally vomited.

As I flew back through the marble hallway strapped to a gurney, I noticed two people.

Rosa stood with a triumphant grin, and leaning, bent over beside her, Brody struggled to give me a thumbs up.

I opened my eyes in a darkened room. I was firmly tucked into a sturdy institutional bed with crisp white sheets and warm blankets. Tubes hung from a bag of clear fluids on a metal pole and disappeared beneath the covers.

I had no idea how long I'd been there, but felt no immediate urge to do anything about it. Closing my eyes, I fell effortlessly into a dreamless sleep.

The next time I awoke, Daniel sat on a chair next to the bed reading a magazine. Flowers had collected in every size, shape and color in each corner of the room.

"Hello, how do you feel?"

"Like I've been run over by a truck, several times. How long have I been here?

"Three days. The doc says you'll be fine. The poison Peggy Jo gave you was a relatively small dose, so they were able to treat it. Turns out she kept her sources close by, right there in her office. You're lucky she chose the toad toxin and not the monkshood."

"That plant was monkshood?" I shivered and looked at all the flowers around me.

I knew I'd have to give or throw away all of them, they remind me too much of the gorgeous blossoms in Peggy Jo's office.

"Yes, and the amount of monkshood in just the sip of tea you took, would've killed you. As it was, the toad poison wasn't a lethal amount." His face was somber, his voice soft and low.

I groaned, closed my eyes, and licked dry, cracked lips.

"Yeah, well I could've done without it, thank you very much."

"Al's been calling the nurse's desk every five minutes to see if you're awake. He can't wait to start yelling at you, and asking questions. By the way, you were brilliant to call 9-1-1."

I managed to heave myself up into a sitting position.

"I was lucky to have Jimmy's old phone with the rubber buttons in my pocket. I could feel them with my fingers without having to see them. I'm so glad I punched the right ones!"

"The dispatcher heard just about everything Peggy Jo said and was able to record the entire event. With Rosa's and Brody's statements, they were able to charge her with Mike Sands' and Tiffany Marsh's murders."

I leaned back quietly on the pillows for a moment.

"So nothing about the fetish, or anything about Charlie?" I heard the wistful note in my voice.

Daniel took my hands in his.

"Don't worry Cali, we'll have plenty of time to find the answers to all our questions."

Seventeen

Monday

The following Monday Daniel drove me home from the hospital. I barely fit into the front passenger seat with the rest of the car stuffed full of flowers and plants. On the way home, we stopped at the Saguaro Gulch Methodist Church and donated every last one of them. If the woman who collected them from us was surprised, she didn't show it.

After reassuring Merry that her human was safe, and home for good, I fell into bed and slept another ten hours. At six in the evening I awoke to a commotion at the front door, and the most amazing, mouth-watering aromas from the kitchen.

"Mom?" Sophie's voice seemed too loud to my still shaky mind.

"Mom? Where are you? Why is Daniel in your kitchen? Why didn't you call me to bring you home?" Sophie shoved open my bedroom door and looked around. I wondered if she was looking for evidence of occupation of her father's side of the bed.

"Sophie, calm down. I'm fine, the doctor says so." She had shown up at the hospital, with a grocery store bouquet, and the promise to move in with me as soon as I got home.

"You know I'd have picked you up! I've got my first suitcase in the car, I'll bring it in and then your . . . friend . . . can leave."

As she whirled around, heading back to the front door, I stopped her.

"Sophie!" My voice must have been harsh enough, because she stopped in her tracks and looked at me with a question in her eyes.

"What? I thought we had this settled." She seemed genuinely surprised. Daniel stood with his back to us, in the kitchen over the stove, with an apron on and a spatula in one hand. I couldn't see his expression.

"I never agreed to have you move in, Sophie. You are certainly welcome to have dinner with us, but I never agreed to anything. You weren't listening to me. And as far as a temporary caretaker, Daniel is all I need right now. You have your own life."

I knew my words were painful, but she'd left me no choice. She hadn't been listening to me since her father had died.

"B-But," she sputtered. "You need me! I can quit my job, take care of you, run errands!" I realized with sudden clarity that something wasn't right.

"Quit your job?" My voice was sharp. "I thought you loved it."

"Oh, Mom! That photography job just wasn't creative enough. When I told my boss, he fired me! I might have missed one, or maybe two, photo sessions." I stared at her.

"OK, three. I missed three appointments. But really! I just want to go out on my own and photograph the desert and the mountain and sell my work to magazines. Artists can't work on a strict schedule and still be amazingly creative."

"So how are you paying your bills?"

Sophie looked uncomfortable.

"I -- I couldn't get another photography job, so I'm working at the Saguaro Gulch Big Box selling cameras. I have my Photography degree, it was the least they could do!"

I sighed.

"Oh, Sophie, we all make mistakes. I'm so glad you've learned that jobs in creative industries are just as structured as any other job, and that you were able to find another one so quickly!"

Sophie blinked. I knew she hadn't learned any such thing, but I gave her the credit anyway.

"Now, will you stay for dinner with us? Daniel is a wonderful cook."

"You're sure you don't need me to move in?"

"Oh, no! I wouldn't dream of being a burden." I smiled inwardly. Two could play this game.

"Well, OK." Sophie was very quiet during dinner, had two helpings of Daniel's Chicken Cacciatore over spaghetti noodles, and snuck shy glances at him from under her eyelashes. As soon as we finished eating, and before cleanup began, she left.

"Think she'll be alright?" Daniel asked as I rinsed, and he loaded the dishwasher.

"Of course. She's stubborn, but she's smart too. When she finally realizes I won't change my mind, she won't waste her time arguing."

Over the next week, I managed to go with Theresa to the doctor's office for her biopsy results. They were negative, but Theresa still hadn't returned to her bubbly self. I wondered if she and Jimmy were still having problems.

"Hi Cali . . . I was wondering if you'd come over and visit tonight . . . I found something I need to show you . . ." One evening she called me, her voice sounded muffled and swollen with tears.

"Sure, what's up?"

"I'm not really sure, but remember when you asked me to ask Jimmy about Mike? He swore he didn't know anything, but he acted really weird afterwards, spent a lot of time rooting around in the garage." Theresa snuffled and then continued. "He wasn't home today, and I was curious, so I went out to the garage . . .just to see if I could figure out what he was doing out there and I found something. You need to come over and tell me what to do before he comes home. I'm scared, Cali!"

"I'll be right over, Theresa. It's just about seven, though, and Daniel's supposed to come by around eight, so I can't stay."

I wondered what was wrong now as I turned the phone off.

"Really, Merry, I feel like everyone thinks they can just dump their problems on me. Why can't people just solve their own stuff? Maybe I should have pushed a little harder to get Theresa to tell me what's going on and suggested a therapist . . . then again, she is my best friend."

Just before seven I scooped up Merry and gave her a hug. Something made me uneasy, and I wasn't taking her with me this time. As I held her I glanced out my picture window towards the canal at the gathering darkness of sunset. Was that a darker mist I saw over the thin ribbon of black water? Setting my puppy gently on the sofa, I gave her a biscuit, checked to make sure the back door was locked and stepped out my front door. I'd been very careful since Merry's near-drowning to make sure all of my doors were locked securely whenever I left the house.

The evening was cooler as I walked carefully down the side-walk toward the Thornberg's driveway. Thank goodness my ankle had healed nicely, and my ribs barely showed any bruising at all.

I knocked at the side kitchen door and Theresa opened it immediately.

"Come on in, Cali." A plate of pumpkin spice cookies and a pot of decaf coffee sat on the table, along with a grubby, plastic grocery bag. She wasn't smiling, but with everything that had happened lately I thought she might just be worn out. I felt a wave of relief as my eyes traveled around the kitchen and I listened for sounds of Jimmy in the house. Nothing.

As we sat and I poured the decaf, Theresa pulled two photos and a small green stone bear from the bag and gently set them on the wooden surface.

Hot coffee splashed dangerously close to the photos as a mug slid from my grasp.

I was startled to see the twin to the bear fetish Daniel now carried. Staring at it, I remembered the strange tingling through my fingers and up my arm the last time I'd touched the bear Merry had found. There was no way I was going to touch this one.

"Theresa, where did you find these?"

"In the garage behind the water heater. These are what you were searching for, right?"

"But we know who killed Mike now, Peggy Jo Baker. She confessed to it."

"Then what's Jimmy doing with these?" Her voice rose an octave.

Hastily wiping my fingers on my jeans I picked up one photograph, and recognized it as the original of the one I'd found in Charlie's shoebox. The faces were clear, and next to Mike Sands stood Jimmy Thornberg.

The second photograph showed Jimmy holding up a tiny carved animal in one hand, and a skull in the other. Who had snapped that picture? My mind was screaming at me.

"I can answer that." A flat, tired voice came from the kitchen doorway.

Jimmy slowly joined us at the table, ignoring the coffee and cookies, shoulders slumped, bags under his eyes.

"Hi Cali." He wasn't smiling.

"H—Hi Jimmy, how are you?"

"Not so good, as it happens."

Theresa snapped to attention and stared at him.

"What do you, mean? What have you done, Jimmy?" The words came out in a whispered rush. "Now that my . . . health scare . . . is over, I thought we'd get back to normal."

What was going on? Looking at her closely, I realized Theresa was nervous, and had been for a long time. Jimmy's unexplained attitude had been wearing on her for a while.

"For you maybe, but not for me." Jimmy sighed. "I've seen how quickly God can take away my most precious thing. You." He stared down at the table.

"You have always been my princess, Theresa, and I've tried to give you everything. But I've failed. I wanted to give you treasure, but I was so obsessed with . . . getting rich . . . I didn't spend enough time with you and . . . and I couldn't have saved you from cancer." He took a deep, shaky breath and rubbed his eyes with his left hand. "Five years ago Mike and I were hired by George Timmons to enlarge the parking up on Devil's Mountain. He was planning to build a visitor center and he wanted us to excavate for the utilities around the edge of the parking area. Get the site ready. On about the third day, we sunk the shovel, and came up with bones. Old, yellow bones." His voice fell to a whisper.

"The back of the skull had been crushed like an egg; someone had smashed the poor guy over the back of the head." Jimmy paused and wiped his eyes again.

"God help us, Mike and me, we robbed the poor bastard. Well, it was me, actually. I practically had to force Mike to take one of the bear carvings. I made him take that photo. For my sins, I was proud of our . . . big discovery! We took the leather pouch buried with him. We thought we'd found treasure! Two stone bears." He poked the carved animal sitting in front of him.

"Mike called the one he took his lucky charm. Ha!" A bark of cynical laughter burst from his lips.

"They've been nothing but trouble! I thought I could sell mine. I'd be famous, and rich, and I'd make a beautiful life for you, Theresa. You'd be so proud of me! But—but that didn't happen. Mike was going to sell his to Brody Marsh, cause we knew he had a collection. He said they were going to meet on the canal, so no one would know, cause it's illegal to steal, sell or buy grave goods. But he died out there, his head stove in just like the skull we found."

Thinking about what I knew now, Peggy Jo must have set up the meeting, and then gone to kill Mike.

Jimmy's hand was shaking now.

"I tried to warn you off, Cali. It's not my fault you wouldn't listen!"

Theresa and I had been hanging on every word, staring at the photographs and the bear fetish. Bits and pieces were beginning to fall into place. Charlie must have known something about what

Jimmy and Mike had done. The note left on my back door suddenly flashed through my mind.

KEEP YOUR NOSE OUT
OR YOU'LL END UP LIKE
YOUR DOG AND YOUR HUSBAND,
DEAD

That meant . . . No!

"It was you? You tied Merry in the canal? You left the note? Jimmy, what did you do to Charlie?"

He pulled his right hand from under the table, and a jolt of fear went through me as he placed a handgun on the table. Where had it come from? He must have had it in his pocket. Did it really matter where it had come from? My mind was shrieking now.

Jimmy took a deep breath and started again.

"I'm going to end it tonight. I'm going to throw this death fetish into the canal. I can't give you riches or fame, or even health. I know now that there's nothing I can do to keep God from taking you from me, Theresa. I can't protect you from cancer, just as Cali couldn't save Charlie. And watching Charlie die an inch at a time was the most horrific thing I've ever seen. Why? Why does God do that?" Not waiting for an answer, he plunged on.

"I can't live with myself, or in this life any longer, and I'm taking Theresa with me. I can't allow her to die of something there's no cure for! And you're coming with us Cali. I tried to warn you off, I didn't mean to hurt either you or Merry, but I misjudged the strength of the water. Charlie gave me a copy of your key, and I was just going to scare you, but you're too nosy! Tonight I was just going to...end Theresa's life in this God-forsaken world, then kill myself, and we'd both be together...and safe. But you just had to keep asking questions, Cali, and now you know, so you're coming with us."

"But . . . But what did you do to Charlie?"

Ignoring me, Jimmy stood, and collecting the gun and the fetish, he motioned us both toward the door.

"Jimmy, there's got to be another way. Just tell your story, it won't be so bad once everyone knows you made a mistake." I pleaded with him. "That's got to be better than murder!"

Theresa was silently crying, tears streaming down her face. Once we were outside, Jimmy grabbed his wife and held her close, the gun buried in her ribs.

"I love you Theresa, I can't leave you here." He whispered into her hair.

"Let Cali go, Jimmy, she doesn't need to be a part of this."

"No, I need to make it a clean sweep. Let's go."

With Theresa held close, he waved me ahead of him.

"If you run, Cali, Theresa leaves this life sooner."

I started out and headed for the canal. It was all I could do to place one foot in front of the other. I needed to know the answer to my question and I wasn't going down without a fight.

The night was growing darker. As I stumbled along I noticed the darker, seething mass of energy in the distance.

The mountain spirit. It knew . . . that death approached.

Jimmy stopped right behind my house. I could hear Merry inside, barking frantically. Did my dog sense danger, or the mountain spirit? I whirled around to face Jimmy, and put my arm around Theresa's shoulders. My back was to the gathering, black, heaving energy.

"Did you kill Charlie, Jimmy? I have to know!" I asked, my voice shaking, not from fear but anger.

Jimmy looked at me sadly.

"I went to visit him. He was just a skeleton, Cali. How could you let him go for so long, without giving him the help he needed? And he told me he was going to tell you about the burial we'd dug up. He'd pieced it all together. But it wasn't our fault! It was Timmons! He was the one who ordered us to re-bury the poor guy, he said he'd take care of it."

"So yeah. I filled a syringe with air and pumped it into his blood stream. I'm pretty sure he died when it reached his heart. He was suffering!"

Jimmy stood forlornly, looking at the two of us, with one hand holding the gun and hanging at his side and the other clutching the tiny twin bear fetish.

Could we run for it? I might've been able to, but Theresa would never make it.

And then a curious thing happened.

A look of complete and utter horror washed over his face as Jimmy looked beyond us. His gun hand slowly came up.

I grabbed Theresa and hit the dirt, dragging her to the ground with me. Gathering my friend into my arms I squeezed my eyes shut and started to pray. The sound of a single shot froze my whole body. I was melded to earth and for a second I couldn't move. Forcing out a slow breath, I quickly peeked behind us, and I saw a black wall of screaming energy. I was looking into the gaping maw of an angry mouth. Petrified, Theresa and I continued to hug each other and the ground, as the sound began to fade. Soon an unnatural quiet blanketed the canal.

Someone had called the police. Sirens began to break the eerie silence. My ears felt numb, like my head was wrapped in cotton, but it seemed neither I nor Theresa had been hit. Risking a glance at Jimmy, I saw the neat round hole in his right temple. The left side of his face and head was gone; the dirt splattered red.

As Al, with Daniel right behind him, hurried forward to rescue me, again, I glanced once more behind me. All I saw was an elderly Native American. He turned, held his hand up in salute, and disappeared.

The second bear fetish was gone.

Several nights later I stood in my kitchen, holding Merry in my arms. I looked out into the clear October night and watched the moonlight slowly move the shadows across my backyard. Closing my eyes, I once more felt Charlie in the room with me. Was it my imagination as his arms embraced us? Merry gave a deep sigh, as the warmth of his love flooded my heart, and slowly washed from my head to my toes.

"Good night, Charlie. I think I can let you go now." I whispered.

"I will always love you, Cali, and I'll be waiting for you on the other side."

Tears gathered in the corner of my eyes as his words faded, and he was gone. Was it my imagination? It didn't matter, I knew Charlie would always be in my heart.

Appendix: Fact or Fiction

All the characters, the mountain spirit and the village of Saguaro Gulch on Devil's Mountain, are figments of my imagination. However, I did live in a small cottage-like home, backing up to a working canal with a desert mountain in the background, on the outskirts of Phoenix, AZ, with my husband, and our miniature dachshund. When we moved there, I'd only known the seasonal color changes of an ever-present canopy of leaves on the East Coast. I couldn't imagine an uglier, less nurturing environment than the desert. Having lived in Arizona now for more than 20 years, I have come to cherish the brilliant oranges, reds, yellows and hot pinks, in both the flamboyant blossoms and sunsets of the American Southwest.

I was surprised to find an astonishing depth of history in the desert, especially around water conservation, and related to the canal behind Cali's home. Many of the current canals around the Valley of the Sun in which Phoenix is located are built on the very real remains of an ancient Native American canal system. Archeologists believe the Hohokam Indians were the first people to design an irrigation system for drinking water and crops in the Arizona-Sonoran Desert, sometime around 600 CE. Their complex canal designs are still considered amazing feats of engineering.

Although the migration of the Silvertree brothers to Phoenix is fictional, many Native Americans suffered displacement at the hands of the American government. The U.S. Government Indian Relocation Act of 1956, a program instituted to forcibly remove

tribal members from their reservations and integrate them into Anglo society, was also designed to disenfranchise an entire cultural
group. Participants were encouraged to leave their reservations,
families, culture, and ancestors and move to any one of a specific
list of approved U.S. cities where they were promised jobs and
housing. In many cases, those promises were not met. Proponents
of the program pointed to the tribal members who acquired education, and then returned to their reservations, and continue to return to apply their educations to the families and tribal societies
they came from. Many others who did not receive the training or
education to survive in the city, found themselves adrift in an unfamiliar, urban society and came to be known as 'Urban Indians'.
Educated or not, those who left their reservations were not fully
accepted back into their cultural society, nor into the predomi-
nantly White cities where they were relocated. Modern Native
Americans are now striving to recapture and maintain their art, history, religion, and languages.

Also by Wendy Fallon

Killing Rose

Cali May's daughter, Sophie, and her new boyfriend, Josh, fall over the body of Dolly Hart, a celebrity 'Jeweler to the Stars' while crawling through the Casa Grande ruins in Coolidge, AZ. At the same time, while waiting for her daughter to re-emerge from the seven-hundred-year-old multi-level mud structure, Cali is visited by a ghost child. Arizona artist, Cali, and Native American Arizona State Park Ranger, Daniel Silvertree, investigate and uncover a decades-old mystery disappearance of a mother and daughter, and a tale of Spanish treasure, sibling jealously, and water theft in the Sonoran Desert. Cali's paranormal ability leads her into forensic art, and she begins providing her paranormal artistic talent to the local Phoenix Police Department.

Magnolia Murders

Arizona artist Cali May, and Native American Arizona State Park Ranger, Daniel Silvertree drive to Sedona, Arizona to enjoy a relaxing week in the high Sonoran Desert at the amazing Magnolia House Bed and Breakfast. Cali is startled to see and hear the ghost of a sobbing woman in the lobby of the guesthouse before she's even shown to their room. Beneath the delightful Sears kit Magnolia floor plan of the 1920s, Cali begins to sense the unnerving presence of hidden secrets. Learning of the disappearance of a child, and the suspicious death of the patriarch who built the house in 1928, Cali realizes that ghosts not only inhabit the structure, but a lifetime of guilt on the part of the current inhabitants is beginning to emerge. Drawing on her paranormal talent and with Daniel's help, Cali unravels the history behind murder.

About the Author

Wendy Fallon, professional writer and artist, lived in Phoenix, AZ for twenty-two years with her husband, three children and a variety of dogs. In 2017 she and her family moved to a beach in Florida.

During the day she works as a technical writer, and evenings and weekends she writes her own stories and creates art. In 2015 Fallon published two books: My Six-Year-Old Inner Artist, Everybody has One! and Your Six-Year-Old Inner Artist Dream Journal, a Workbook, about personal creativity. Cali May Mysteries is her first three-book series of Southwest, paranormal, murder mysteries, in which California (Cali) May solves cold and current murders while learning to trust her controversial talent, seeing spirits.

Where to find Wendy:
Website: WendyFallon.com
Facebook: Wendy Wickham Fallon
Twitter: @WAFallon